The Devil's Gunhand

The Devil's Gunhand

A Shawn Starbuck Western

Ray Hogan

Thorndike Press • **Chivers Press**
Thorndike, Maine USA   **Bath, England**

This Large Print edition is published by Thorndike Press, USA and by Chivers Press, England.

Published in 2000 in the U.S. by arrangement with Golden West Literary Agency.

Published in 2000 in the U.K. by arrangement with Golden West Literary Agency.

U.S. Hardcover 0-7862-2980-2 (Western Series Edition)
U.K. Hardcover 0-7540-4370-3 (Chivers Large Print)
U.K. Softcover 0-7540-4371-1 (Camden Large Print)

The text of this Large Print edition is unabridged.
Other aspects of the book may vary from the original edition.

Set in 16 pt. Plantin by Al Chase.

Printed in the United States on permanent paper.

British Library Cataloguing-in-Publication Data available

Library of Congress Cataloging-in-Publication Data

Hogan, Ray, 1908–
    The devil's gunhand : a Shawn Starbuck western / by Ray
Hogan.
        p.   cm.
    ISBN 0-7862-2980-2 (lg. print : hc : alk. paper)
    1. Starbuck, Shawn (Fictitious character) — Fiction.
2. Large type books. I. Title.
PS3558.O3473 D45 2000
    813′.54—dc21
                                                        00-064792

The Devil's Gunhand

1

Starbuck settled back as the girl sitting opposite him turned to face the man who had paused beside her. Blond, brown-eyed, she possessed a distinct beauty despite the hard veneer of cosmetics that masked her features.

"Yeh?"

"Was wondering — you tying in with this bird permanent, Nella? Been hanging around him ever since he hit town."

"Maybe," she replied indifferently, brushing at a wrinkle in the lap of her red and black spangled dress.

The cowhand shrugged, glanced around the saloon. It was shortly after midday and patronage was light, only a dozen or so men present.

"Sorta forget your old friends mighty fast, don't you?"

"Move on," Nella said coolly, and resumed her position at the table.

Starbuck watched the man drift off into the room. He shook his head. "Not smart, cutting yourself off like that. Expect to be pulling out today or tomorrow."

The girl frowned. "So soon?"

"Got to. Luck wasn't running my way last night and those last few hands of poker cost me. I'm pretty well down to rock bottom far as cash is concerned. Means I have to scare myself up a job."

Starbuck paused, looked across the saloon to a corner table where several men were carrying on a loud conversation. Their words were harsh and the gathering had all the earmarks of oncoming violence. Other customers had fallen silent and were watching, as was Pete Whitcomb, the owner.

"I've got a few dollars laid back if you —"

"Obliged," Starbuck cut in with a shake of his head, "but I'm not about to let you or anybody else stake me. Coming up broke's nothing new. I've had to rustle myself a job quite a few times before. One reason finding my brother's taking me so long, I expect."

Nella made no reply, again fell to fingering her dress. Then, "Shawn, where will you go?"

"On west, or maybe south into Mexico. One direction's as good as another since I've got no good idea where Ben is. Kind of a hit-and-miss proposition."

She stirred wearily. "I wish you wouldn't go —"

A sudden crash interrupted her words. One of the men at the corner table had toppled backward. The fall had broken the back off his chair, and in going over his booted feet had caught the edge of the table, dumping its contents and almost upsetting it. With the help of his friends, all laughing and shouting, the puncher was being righted.

"That bunch there've had about all the liquor they can handle," Starbuck said. "Time Whitcomb was putting them out."

"He won't. That's Yancey Lingo and his crowd. Nobody tells the Lingos what to do."

"Lingo," Shawn repeated the name. "Rufus Lingo. Seems I've heard of him."

"He's Yancey's pa. Owns about half the town and a big ranch fifteen miles or so north of here — and there's talk he aims to be the next governor of the Territory. Yancey's his pride and joy. Gets away with anything."

"Which one's him?"

"The fancy vest and sharp face. Other three hang around him all the time, licking up after him, saying yes and no whenever they're expected to. Young one with the cotton hair is Billy Joe Spicer. The mean-looking redhead is Red Davis. Other one with the big shoulders is Harley Greer. He's a gunman from somewheres — hired on by

Rufus to see that his boy never gets what's coming to him."

"Fine company —"

"Way Rufus wants it, I guess. Like I said, Yancey can do no wrong far as he's concerned and he wants that bunch of hard cases around to look after him. . . . You wouldn't be willing to head east for Texas, would you?"

Starbuck stirred. "Just came from there. Was on a trail drive from the Big Springs country to Dodge City. Things didn't go just the way they should have, and by the time I was through with the deal, I felt like I was being let out of a jail."

"So you wound up here, blowing your wages and coming out broke —"

"Something a man has to do every now and then. You thinking about going to Texas?"

The girl shrugged. "I've been here about two years. Time I moved on. Texas is usually a place where you can make money." She hesitated, smiled. "It won't have to be Texas. I wouldn't mind heading west, or maybe down into Mexico — as long as it was with you."

Shawn studied the girl closely. He'd never had a female traveling companion and reckoned it would have certain definite advantages but guessed it wouldn't be a good idea.

"Appreciate the idea, and the offer, but I expect I'd best pass it up. Could be I'll find myself a job somewhere nearby, anyway."

"Was just a thought," Nella said with a sigh. "You didn't learn anything here about this brother you're looking for?"

He shook his head, began to toy with the empty whiskey glass on the table, twirling it between a thumb and forefinger. "Asked around, nobody can remember seeing him. Still have to talk to the sheriff about it."

"Be your best bet. Sam Culvert's a good lawman even if he is a bit old. If your brother ever came through here he'll know it."

"You acquainted with him?"

"Some. He's about the only man in town that's not walking on his knees to Rufus Lingo."

Shawn's eyebrows lifted. "That's a change. Usually a town's big wheel's got the law working for him."

"That's what Rufus would like, only Sam won't go for it — and everybody knows Lingo's out to get rid of him on account of it and replace him with somebody he can run. I've heard it said that Sam Culver has something on Rufus."

11

"Being a sheriff means he's elected by the people of the whole county and not appointed, like a town marshal. Lingo'll have to wait until election time comes and then get folks to vote his way."

"Which they'll probably do. Rufus Lingo swings a lot of weight."

Shawn's attention drifted to the far corner of the saloon. Yancey and his friends had procured a new bottle of whiskey and were passing it around noisily.

"Doubt if his son's carrying on is going to earn him much support," he said drily as the younger Lingo, twisting about on his chair, began to pour liquor on the head of a man sitting at an adjoining table.

"Won't make any difference. Yancey's like bad weather. He's something folks just have to put up with."

The puncher Lingo was dousing with whiskey had leaped to his feet, was mopping at his eyes with a bandana while angry words were pouring from his lips. Yancey, leaning back in his chair, was roaring with laughter. Spicer and Red Davis were joining in, but the hard-featured Greer was eyeing the man narrowly.

Whitcomb crossed to the table hurriedly, carrying a towel. He added his efforts to those of the aggrieved rider while he said something in a quick, hopeful manner. The puncher shrugged, settled into his chair. Harley Greer relaxed.

"Seems nobody told that cowhand about putting up with Yancey's little jokes," Starbuck murmured.

"He knows now. Pete's given him the word."

"Must be a stranger."

"Expect he is. Probably just passing through. You decided yet when you'll pull out?"

Shawn, gaze straying around the big room, touching the wagonwheel chandeliers with their circle of lamps, the scatter of tables and chairs, the hushed patrons, the bar with its dusty mirror and row of bottles, stirred restlessly.

It was good to be off the trail, under a roof, in a place where there were people, where he could enjoy the friendly sounds and smells of everyday living. That he was a footloose wanderer with no foreseeable permanent ties weighed heavily upon him at times.

"Morning will be soon enough."

Nella smiled happily. "Fine. Maybe by then I can change your mind about taking me along —"

A shout went up from the corner. Yancey

13

had risen, was again dumping whiskey on the head of the man at the next table. The puncher came upright, curses bursting from his mouth. He wheeled, reached for the pistol on his hip. There was a sudden, shocking blast as Greer drew and fired, filling the saloon with rebounding echoes and a surge of smoke. The puncher staggered, clawed at his shoulder, tripped over a chair and fell. Greer raised his weapon for a second shot. Lingo flung out an arm, stayed him.

"My turn!" he yelled and reached for his own gun. "It's going to be me teaching this saddlebum a lesson!"

Starbuck was on his feet and across the room in half a dozen strides. His right hand stabbed forward, fingers wrapping about Lingo's weapon and wrenching it free. In almost the same motion he spun, drove a balled fist into the belly of Harley Greer, effectively stalling the gunman's attempt to use his pistol again.

Taut, Starbuck stepped back. Yancey was staring at him fixedly with hate-filled eyes, his mouth working angrily. Nearby Greer, buckled forward, was sucking for breath. Spicer and Davis hung poised, features intent as if awaiting the proper moment to strike.

Shawn considered them coldly. "Whatever you're thinking — forget it!" he snapped.

The shoulders of the pair went down slowly. Spicer swallowed noisily and Davis looked away. Shawn felt a hand on his arm, drew aside as Whitcomb and several others crowded over the wounded man sprawled on the floor. The saloonkeeper assisted him to his feet.

"Just a little hole in the shoulder," he said. "You get yourself over to Doc Grey's — he'll fix you up. It's down the street a couple of doors. I'll take care of the paying —"

"No," Starbuck cut in flatly. "That's Lingo's chore." He faced Yancey. "Fork it over. Reckon five dollars ought to handle it."

Lingo did not stir. Starbuck rode out ten long seconds and then laid the man's pistol upon the table, an open invitation to pick up the weapon, use it, plain in his eyes.

Yancey hesitated for another brief period, and then dug into his pocket. Bringing forth a handful of coins, he dropped the required number of silver dollars beside the gun.

"There it is," he said in a strained voice, "but, mister, I ain't forgetting this! Ain't nobody ever shoved me around."

Shawn gathered up the money, stacking

15

the coins one on top of the other in his fingers, and passed them to the stranger, who bobbed his head and started for the door.

"Always a first time for everything," he murmured.

"And a last," Lingo declared savagely. "You're lagging for the boneyard when you cross me! I'll —"

"Ease off, Yancey!" a voice called from the far side of the crowd that had gathered around the men. "You ain't doing nothing — and I've had just about all I aim to take from you!"

2

Starbuck glanced at the speaker, an elderly, graying man with pale eyes, hooked nose, and a stringy mustache that matched a raggedly cut beard. He was somewhat below average height, but there was a cool competence in his manner that bolstered the authority indicated by the star he was wearing. This would be Sam Culver, Shawn realized.

"Keep out of this, Sheriff!" Yancey snarled. "It ain't none of your butt-in."

"Anytime I hear a gunshot I make it my butt-in," the lawman replied briskly as he shouldered his way through the gathering of bystanders. Halting beside Starbuck, he favored all with a sharp look. "What happened here?"

There was no volunteered reply from the crowd. Shawn shrugged. Rufus Lingo's hold on the town of Kennesaw was even tighter than he'd been led to believe. But the man meant nothing to him.

"Yancey was hoorawing that man you saw headed for the doc's. Fellow objected and Greer shot him. Yancey was going to finish him off, so I took a hand."

Interest narrowed Culver's eyes as he swept Starbuck from hat to boot. Cocking his head to one side, he said: "That so? Don't you know you ain't supposed to horn in on Yancey when he's having what he figures is fun?"

The mocking tone was not lost on Shawn. His shoulders stirred. "Sure didn't —"

"Something you'll be paying for later," Lingo said coldly.

Starbuck's voice was equally flat. "Welcome to try collecting anytime you're of a mind."

"Expect you'll be the one that's doing the paying, Yancey!" Culver stated, his craggy features hardening. "I've put up with you about as long as I aim to. You ain't nothing but trouble — been that way ever since you was born, and I'm mighty damned tired of it!"

"Do tell!" Lingo said with a scornful grin. "Now, just what do you figure you can do about it?"

"A-plenty. Been looking into a couple of your cute tricks, and if things work out, I'll be jugging you on some charges you won't squirm out of."

"Charges? What the hell you yakking about, old man?"

"Roping that hired hand of Charlie May's and letting a horse drag him till he was most dead, for one thing."

"Aw, we was only funning —"

"Funning! He maybe's going to die from it! And then there's that Mex girl that works for the Kilibrides. Shape you left her in after you and your bunch got through —"

"She was only a Mex. Hell, we —"

"Only a Mex! What's that mean? You think she ain't a human and entitled to be treated same as other folks? Then there's that little jag of steers of Abe Foreman's that just up and disappeared one night right after you and them three that sides you was seen on his place —"

"You calling me a rustler?" Yancey demanded, his voice high-pitched with anger.

"Not yet, but I'm hoping to, and if I come up with some proof you're going to jail for it. Just because you're Rufus Lingo's boy don't cut no hay with me. Far as I'm concerned you're nothing but another outlaw needing to be put in the pen for a spell, or maybe even hung!"

"You try saddling me with something, and by God, I'll —"

"You won't do nothing, boy. You'll take what you got coming to you like every other owlhoot that's been caught breaking the law. Goes for the rest of you, too," the lawman said, pausing to touch the three men beside Lingo with his glance. "Far as I can see you're just as guilty as him."

Yancey had recovered his composure to some extent. He looked at his friends, ranged around him in a small half-circle. The features of Billy Joe and Davis were drawn, reflected some degree of alarm. Greer showed only a sullen defiance and hatred. He had been up against the law before, Shawn concluded, had no use for any man who wore a badge.

Lingo shifted his eyes, swung them over the oddly silent crowd of bystanders. "You're just doing a lot of talking. You ain't got no proof — and nobody'll give you any."

"I'll find it, probably," the old sheriff replied. "Take this little ruckus you started here. Seems I got one man seeing it that ain't scared of talking. Him swearing to me that you shot down that fellow —"

"Was self-defense," Greer said. "Went for his iron. I beat him to pulling the trigger."

Culver turned to Shawn. "That right?"

"Could be called that," Starbuck answered. "Man started to draw on Yancey. Greer stopped him."

"Then what?"

"Lingo was going to shoot him again — while he was on the floor. Teach him a lesson, he said."

"Sounds like Yancey all right. What come next?"

"I stopped him."

The old lawman grinned, faced the crowd. "Sure mighty good to have one man in the place."

There was no response from the onlookers. The fear and power of Rufus Lingo, although not present, was like a dark, menacing shadow in the saloon.

"All right, I'm calling it self-defense and letting it go at that, but it wouldn't ever've happened if you hadn't been acting smart. And it could've wound up with that stranger getting killed — but I reckon that wouldn't've meant nothing to any of you."

"Was a fool to go for his gun," Greer said.

"Not exactly. Any man's got the right to stand up for himself when he's being put upon by some jackass like you —"

"Easy, Sheriff."

"Don't go threatening me! I've been dealing with you two-bit gunhands for plenty of years and you plain don't scare me none. Same goes for you, Yancey. Maybe you and your pa've got everybody else around here buffaloed, but not me, and when I come up with the proof I'm after I'm going to put an end to this funning, as you call it, and lock you away where you won't be hurting nobody for a long spell!"

Starbuck, standing back from the table, arms crossed over his chest, watched the expression on Harley Greer's face harden. Yancey was showing no change, nor were Spicer and Red Davis. Only the gunman was reacting to the harsh words and tongue-lashing Culver was administering. Shawn frowned. The lawman was pushing hard — possibly too hard.

"Now, I'm serving notice on all of you for the last time," the sheriff continued. "I'm out to get you and the way I see it my chances are mighty good. It won't be for some smart-alec stunt you've pulled, neither; it'll be for something that'll earn you some years behind bars, or maybe even a hanging — and that's what it'll be if that hired hand of May's croaks."

Yancey Lingo's face paled. "Hell, he wasn't hurt that bad."

"You don't think so? Ask Doc Grey. Don't take my word for it. Doc'll tell you it don't look good."

Billy Joe's voice suddenly broke through the lawman's words. "I told you, Yancey! Told you we ought'nt to go —"

"Shut up, kid," Greer snapped. "The old man's just talking to hear himself rattle. He ain't about to go bucking Yancey's pa, no matter what."

Sam Culver grinned bleakly. "You think I ain't? Well, just so's you'll get it straight in your head, I got the whole thing squared away with Tom Spain, the U.S. marshal in Prescott. He knows what's been going on and that I'm digging up the proof I need so's we'll have a case when the right time comes. All I've got to do is drop word to him and he'll be here quick."

"You won't never get the chance to do that," Greer yelled and reached for his pistol.

Starbuck, gauging the gunman's mental capacities accurately, moved in that same fraction of time. His left hand swept down, came up fast with the forty-five he carried. The heavy weapon rapped sharply, filling the room again with echoes and swirling smoke. Greer, pistol half clear of its leather holster, slammed back against the wall behind him as the bullet drove into his body. He hung there briefly and then fell forward across the table.

The stunned silence held for a long breath. A voice finally gasped, "My God!"

Shawn, the act laying its restraint upon

him, stood motionless. He had reacted automatically, instantly, and without thought when the gunman had made his move to shoot down the lawman. Vaguely he heard the suppressed comments of the crowd, some men remarking on the speed with which he'd drawn and fired, others at the bald fact of killing.

"All right, it's done with." The words of Sam Culver were low and strong. "Yancey, I'm ordering you and the rest of your bunch to get out of here. Reckon you see now what your tomfoolery can lead to — somebody gets hurt, or killed. Now, move on, else I'll jug you for being the real cause of this."

Lingo, with Spicer and the redheaded Davis close behind, walked out from back of the table and through the crowd, which fell away to admit them. At the batwings Lingo paused. His face was taut. "I ain't done with you, Sheriff, or with that gunslinger you got siding you! Way I see it, was all a put-up job. You brought him here, had him hanging around just waiting for a chance to use that iron of his — but I aim to square things. You can bet your bottom dollar on that!"

"Guess again, Yancey," Culver replied, smiling. "I don't even know the man. You just run up against somebody that ain't knuckling under to you and your pa. Keep moving."

The three men passed on through the doorway and were lost to view. The lawman turned to the crowd, now slowly pulling off into the saloon.

"Couple of you, grab hold of Greer, lug him over to the undertakers for me."

There was no sign that anyone heard. The men continued to drift off, clearly wanting nothing to do with the incident. Starbuck shrugged.

"Never mind, Sheriff," he said, sliding his pistol into its holster. "I'll carry him. You lead the way."

3

Someone had procured a blanket from one of the second-floor bedrooms and laid it over Greer. Shawn, kneeling, rolled the gunman's body into it, slung it over his shoulder, and wheeled to follow Culver into the street.

Word of the shooting had preceded them. As they stepped into the open a small crowd faced them. Starbuck was instantly aware of the hostility the town harbored for the old lawman. It was strange. Most places would have welcomed, or at least little noted, the elimination of a gunman; here in Kennesaw it was as if a hero of some proportion had been slain.

Silent, he followed the tight-lipped lawman down the broad, dusty lane to a small clapboard structure that sat back and somewhat apart from its neighbors. A simple white sign bearing the black letters UNDERTAKER was nailed across its front.

It appeared wholly deserted, but when they entered to be met by a small man with nervous, birdlike movements, Starbuck saw that there were two other persons present.

One was a tall, darkly clad man with a large shock of bushy brown hair capping a skull of a head and deep-set, snapping eyes placed close together in a narrow face.

With him was a girl of around his own age, Shawn reckoned. She was exceptionally pretty in a quiet, serene way, with dark hair, blue eyes, and a figure not entirely concealed by the severe, staid dress she wore. There was the look of utter submissiveness upon her features, but as he came into the shadowy, ill-smelling room and laid his burden upon a long, narrow table, interest appeared to stir through her.

"Greer," Culver said to the undertaker and then nodded coolly to the tall man. "Howdy, Reverend. You, too, Miss Sarah."

"Greer!" the minister echoed in a booming voice. "A man, not just a name! A living, breathing man — the work of Almighty God — laid low by a killer!"

The sheriff sighed, wagged his head. "You got it wrong, Reverend. Greer's the killer. Just come up against another man that was quicker'n him. Good thing, too, else it'd be me laying there instead of him. . . . Got this fellow here to thank for that."

The minister swung his crackling gaze to Shawn. "You? You killed this man?"

Starbuck nodded, aware that the girl had

27

not taken her glance from him. He smiled faintly. There was the suggestion of response upon her perfectly shaped lips.

"This is Reverend York," Culver said, making an introduction. "The young lady's his daughter, Sarah. Folks, I'd like for you to meet —" The lawman hesitated, frowned as he looked at Shawn. "Hell's fire, I don't even know what you're called!"

"Starbuck. Shawn Starbuck."

"My friend Shawn Starbuck," the sheriff completed. "Like I said, if it wasn't for him I'd be dead. Greer aimed to kill me for sure."

"I have word that it was otherwise!" York boomed. "I was told this man Greer was provoked into using his pistol so that he could be murdered."

"You was told wrong, Parson," Culver said calmly. "You ask the right people and maybe they'll tell you different if they've got the sand to be truthful. Who'd you hear that from — Yancey Lingo?"

York bobbed his head. "From him. I met him on my way here. This poor man was a friend of his."

"Yancey's lying as usual. He tell you that this here poor man you're moaning about shot another fellow during a ruckus in the Wagonwheel Saloon, and then Yancey hisself was about to put another bullet into the same man? Would've, too, if Starbuck hadn't took a hand."

"That seems unlikely —"

"I don't give a hoot what it seems like to you, Reverend! You been closing your eyes to the things Yancey Lingo's been pulling around here ever since his pa built that church for you! When're you going to get some sense and see the Lingos for what they are?"

"You are wrong, Sheriff Culver. The Lingos are fine, upstanding people. The boy is, well, mischievous, as are most all boys. Neither of them deserve the persecution being visited upon them by you."

"Persecution!" Culver shouted, suddenly beside himself. "I'm doing my job, and if you want to call that —"

"Philistines — both of you! Men who wear guns are ever ready to shoot down some unfortunate creature, rob him of the precious gift of life the Almighty has given him."

"Aw, hell," the lawman muttered in disgust and turned away.

Anger was stirring through Shawn at York's unreasonable attitude. He studied the minister. "I don't hold with killing," he said quietly, "but I think you'd best go back

29

to your Bible. Few things you ought to get straight."

"The Bible!" York repeated scornfully. "What does a man like you know of the Bible?"

"Folks brought me up on it, and after listening to you, I'd say they understood it a lot better than you."

York colored. "Don't you lecture me on the Bible! I've spent a lifetime —"

"Maybe so, but the way you're talking you still don't know what it's all about."

"I know that you've taken a man's life, have probably killed others. You are the devil's gunhand, doing his bidding in defiance of the laws of the Almighty —"

The mortician hovering nearby was sweating nervously. "Gentlemen — gentlemen —"

Starbuck stepped back. There was little point in arguing with a man like York, one who could not and would not see any side of a question other than his own. The thought came to him: was the man sincere in his contention, or was he, as Sam Culver had declared earlier, making a strong stand for the Lingos because of the family's generosity to the church?

He glanced again to Sarah York, demure and silent in the stuffy room. She appeared unaffected by the rantings of her father, likely had hardened herself to such displays. Sarah would not have much of a life, he supposed.

"Was you knowing the things I do about the Lingos, you'd not be talking up so strong," Culver said, once again calm. "That Yancey's trouble of the worst kind, has been ever since he was big enough to milk a goat. I could tell you a few things he's done that'd curl your whiskers, only with your daughter around, I dassen't."

York drew up stiffly. "I'll not hear him bad-mouthed. He's a spirited boy and harmless pranks —"

"Harmless? You know what he done to Charlie May's hired hand — him and that bunch that runs with him?"

"I'll not listen to idle talk, especially when it comes from a man who is well known to hate the family, to resent them because they have done well in God's sight —"

"Dammit to hell!" Culver exploded, and then looked hastily at Sarah. "Excuse me," he said and again turned away. "Ain't no use jawing with you, Ahab. You always was bullheaded and narrow-minded." The lawman shifted his attention to the undertaker. "I'll send Doc over to do his coronering, Henry. Just leave Greer laying

31

there like he is till he has his look."

The nervous little man bobbed his head. "Fine. Now, as to the burying —"

"If you don't find enough cash on him to pay for it, the county'll make up the difference. Ought to be up to the Lingos. Rufus was paying him wages to look after Yancey."

The lawman moved toward the doorway, ignoring the hard, straight gaze of York. He paused as the minister's voice reached out to him.

"You'd best repent, mend your ways — both of you! Those who live by the sword shall perish by it, thus saith the Lord!"

"Reckon so," Culver replied indifferently, "but you ought to be mighty thankful to your Lord that there's somebody around like Starbuck and me to keep wolves like Greer there out of your fold, else you wouldn't have nobody to preach to. . . . Maybe even you wouldn't be here because that mouth of yourn likely would've got you killed a long time ago."

Sam Culver moved on. Shawn, glancing at the girl, smiled, touched the brim of his hat with a forefinger, and followed the older man out into the sunlight.

4

They halted on the board sidewalk at the end of the street. The crowd that had gathered in front of Pete Whitcomb's Wagonwheel Saloon had dispersed, and likely things within the structure had returned to normal. The town itself also seemed to have resumed its torpid, summertime tenor.

"You be in a hurry?" Culver asked, sleeving away the sweat on his lined face.

"Not specially."

"Good. Sure would like to do some talking with you. In my office."

Shawn nodded. "Figured to drop by before I rode out, anyway, ask you about my brother. Be as good a time as any."

"Fine," the lawman said and struck off down the walk. Shawn fell in beside him, aware of the glances they drew from persons on the street and inside the stores as they passed. The thought came again to him that Sam Culver was a man pretty much alone in his town.

They reached the jail, a little more than midway along the opposing rows of buildings and homes, and turned into it. The lawman paused briefly to glance at a low brick-fronted structure a bit farther on, and opposite. Lettering on the window stated: RUFUS LINGO INVESTMENTS & LAND BROKER. Four horses were tied to the hitchrack and a balding, sharp-faced man with neatly trimmed mustache and wearing a business suit stood in the doorway.

"That Lingo?" Starbuck asked.

"That's him — the old he-coon hisself."

"Looks like a politician."

"Just what he is, and a slick one. Got a finger in about every pie in the county, and some that ain't. Ranch of his is said to be one of the best in the Territory."

"Can see why he swings a big club."

"Club's sure the right word for it!" Culver said, moving on into the small, stuffy office area that occupied the forepart of the structure. "I reckon there ain't hardly a man in this town that don't know how crooked he is but ain't saying or doing nothing about it because Rufe's got a string tied to him for some reason."

"Like Ahab York."

"Like him. Rufus was plenty smart there. Ahab started out doing his preaching in an old store building at the edge of town. Rufe quick seen how he could grab hisself an edge and stepped in and built a regular church for Ahab.

"Ever since he's been sort've adding to things, them colored-glass windows, them pews instead of the benches folks was setting on. Some time back Rufe let it get mentioned that he was thinking about buying an organ so's they wouldn't have to keep using the old piano Pete Whitcomb donated when he got a new one. Doings like that kind of keep Rufe Lingo on top."

"And cause folks around here to overlook the things he and Yancey do that aren't exactly right," Shawn finished.

"That's it," Culver said, sinking into the chair behind his desk while motioning Starbuck to another. "Them two can dang nigh get away with anything."

Shawn settled down. "Back there in the saloon it sounded to me like you were about to put a stop to some of Yancey's hellraising."

"I am. Figure I've finally got just about enough proof, if things keep going right, to throw him into the pen and keep him there — in spite of what Rufus will try to do. Big problem I've had all along is getting something bad enough on him — and something that I can prove. At the same time it's got to be something his pa can't buy him out of.

"Tom Spain, he's the U.S. marshal,

knows all about it, and he's been sort've helping me along, advising me, I reckon you'd say. Problem is, being sheriff means I've got the whole county to look out for, not just this here one town, so the job of doing that and working on nailing down Yancey's kept me busier than a one-armed man shearing sheep. Reason I brung you here to do some talking."

The old lawman paused, studied Starbuck intently. Then, "Ahab right — calling you a gunslinger?"

Shawn frowned. It was an appellation he'd never cared for.

"Don't mean no offense," Culver said, smiling. "Just that I'd like to know. Way you handled that sixshooter you're a-wearing —"

"Not a hired gun," Starbuck said flatly. "Never was and I'm not interested in that kind of a job. Been times when I've made a living with it — being a town marshal or a deputy or maybe doing guard work."

"I see. What I was hoping for. Now, don't take no offense at this either, but is there any wanted dodgers out on you?"

"No —"

"Fine. Makes it easy to offer you a job. Be real proud to have you as my deputy."

"Been wondering why you didn't have one —"

Culver snorted. "Why? For the plain reason there ain't nobody that'd take the job! All scared to buck the Lingos. They'd get rid of me, too; would've a long time ago, I expect, only I'm elected and don't have to depend on the town council to appoint me."

"Was told about that," Starbuck said, thinking about the offer.

Culver misread the hesitation. "You won't have no hard job to do. Just hang around town, sort of keep an eye on the usual things — drunks mostly. Long as there's a lawman handy the hard cases behave themselves. Main thing, it'll turn me loose so's I can work on jailing Yancey. Just ain't had enough time, what with the rest of the county to look after, too."

Starbuck nodded thoughtfully. After a time he faced Culver squarely. "There anything personal in this Lingo thing — more than him breaking the law, I mean?"

The sheriff swore. "Lot of folks think maybe there is and I reckon they got a right to — but it sure'n hell ain't so. Happens I ain't for letting Yancey get away with things another man would get jailed for — and he's growing worse. Sooner or later somebody's going to get killed by his foolishness — maybe already has.

"And then there's Rufus. Know a few

37

things about him that ain't good. He needs stopping, too. He ever gets what he's working for this whole Territory'll be in a bad way."

"Why?"

"He's grabbing onto land, buying, leasing, stealing too, I expect, all over the country. Wants to have control of every danged acre he can so's he can sell out to some big mining and cattle companies — syndicates, they call them. It works out the way he's planning, this here won't be no Territory, it'll just be a bunch of outfits owned by outsiders putting damned little in and taking everything out."

"There any proof of that?"

"Not the kind a man can show, since it's all being done real quiet and under-the-table-like, but I found out from a fellow back East — one of them stock sellers. Done him a favor once when he was out here. Was him that give me the lowdown and told me how to look things up in the county records. Done it and he was sure right."

Starbuck shrugged. He wasn't sure if there was anything illegal or detrimental in Rufus Lingo's activities or not. Yancey, however, was a different matter; he had firsthand knowledge of him and there was no doubt in his mind that the younger Lingo was dangerous and should be curbed.

"Deputy job don't pay too grand," Shawn heard Culver say. "Fifty a month with a shack out back to live in."

Accepting the job offer would void the need to move on and find the work he needed to rebuild his finances, and Kennesaw was a pretty good town; it wouldn't be such a bad place to hang around for a few months — at least until the first of the year.

Too, he'd like to get better acquainted with Sarah York, make her understand that he didn't go around shooting men whenever the whim overtook him. But getting to know her could be a chore, considering the way her father felt and the fact that she appeared to be so totally subservient to him.

"What do you say?" There was a hopefulness in the old lawman's tone. It was almost childish in quality. "Sure would be doing me a mighty big favor — not that you ain't already done me one I'll find hard to pay back."

"No need for that."

"Could be you're figuring I'm too much of a talker, that I rattle on a powerful lot. Been told that a few times, and I reckon maybe it's true — but when I meet a man I cotton to I sort of cut loose. Ain't no need for you to fret about that, howsomever, 'cause I don't aim to be around much."

Shawn made no reply. Sam Culver was a bit long on words, he had to admit, but such was understandable. A lawman's job, by its very nature, made for a lonely life, and close friends were few in number.

"That won't bother me any," Starbuck said finally. "I'll take the offer if you don't mind me quitting after a few months."

Culver leaped to his feet, a broad smile on his seamy face. "That's jake with me! Need you now. Later on things'll've sloped off." Jerking open a drawer of the desk he probed about, procured a star upon which were the words DEPUTY SHERIFF. "Stand up and raise your hand," he directed.

Starbuck complied. The lawman, still smiling, said, "You swear to uphold the laws of the Territory of Arizona, so help you God?"

Shawn nodded.

"Say it —"

"I do."

"Then right here and now I make you a deputy sheriff of this county," Culver said, and reaching forward, pinned the star on Shawn's shirt pocket. Extending his hand, he added, "I'm mighty glad to make you welcome.

"Now, there was something you was wanting to talk to me about — your brother, I recollect it was."

Starbuck, looking past the lawman through the open doorway, shook his head. "Guess that'll have to wait a bit, Sheriff. We're about to have company — the Lingos."

5

Sam Culver's pale eyes flickered briefly. His lips tightened into a smug smile. "Figured that," he murmured and sank into the chair behind the desk.

Shawn stepped back into a corner of the room, folded his arms across his chest, and leaned against the wall. There was this much to be said for Rufus Lingo — he was a man well supplied with brass and one not in the least intimidated by the law or its representative.

He stepped through the doorway, halted, Yancey at his side. Beyond him the long shadows of closing day were striking across the dusty street, while the amber of failing sunlight tinted the store windows and spread warmly over the land.

"Culver, I'm warning you again — quit riding my boy!"

Lingo came straight to the point. His features were set, his manner stiff, but he was in absolute control of himself. Smirking, Yancey looked on in silence, wholly confident in the reassuring presence of his parent.

The sheriff cocked his head to one side, studied the man before him. "Little late to be saying that," he drawled. "Your boy's done tore his britches."

"Only according to what you say. Yancey tells me there's no truth in what you accuse him of."

"There's proof," Culver said bluntly. "Right time comes I'll show it."

"Doubt that — and meanwhile you're going to keep on ragging him, trying to force him into a spot where you can kill him."

"No, can't say as that's come to my mind."

"It has and you know it! Yancey told me how you jockeyed Harley Greer into drawing his gun so's your hired killer could shoot him down."

The lawman's brows lifted. "Had a hunch he'd tell you some kind of a crazy yarn like that. Lying comes mighty easy to him."

"I believe him," Rufus Lingo said flatly and shifted his attention to Shawn. "You're the one who did it, I expect." He paused, shook his head. "Got your reward, I see. Made you his deputy."

"Was looking for a job. This one was open so I took it," Starbuck replied coldly.

"A bit strange. Plenty of men around here that could use the work —"

"Plenty around," Culver snapped, "only none of them had guts enough to hire on — on account of you!"

"I've got nothing to do with it — but that's neither here nor there. Point is, I want you to lay off Yancey. I'm telling you, in fact, and if you don't —"

"You ain't telling me nothing, Rufe!" Culver said, coming to his feet. "You ain't never been able to, and you ain't never going to. Yancey's in bad trouble and I aim to see he pays for it. You figure you can stop me from doing my job, then you go right ahead and crack your whip!"

Lingo listened quietly, face expressionless. When the lawman had finished he nodded slowly. "All right, if that's how it's to be, I'll see what can be done about it, and you know that's plenty. I won't have you and your gunslinger hounding my boy, trying to force him into the same spot as you did Greer."

"Up to him," Culver said evenly. "He straightens up and acts decent, then that time ain't likely to come. But if he ever draws on me or my deputy you can figure on burying him."

Rufus Lingo's shoulders were stiff against the doorway's rectangle of soft light. "I consider that a threat."

"Nope," the sheriff said, "it's a promise."

Yancey, at last breaking his silence, reached for his father's arm. "You see, Pa? You see how it is? He's plain out to get me, no matter what. Hell, I ain't done nothing that nobody else —"

"Nothing!" Culver exploded. "You mean near killing that Mex gal was nothing? And turning a half-broke bronc loose to drag that hired hand of May's was nothing? And them steers of —"

"Nothing but pranks, Sheriff," the elder Lingo broke in his tone changing. "Why, we all went through a time when we pulled foolish tricks like that. You can't call those things a crime — if you did you'd have to lock up two-thirds of the men in this town."

"Reckon you'll not find any man around here or anywhere else that'd go as far as Yancey's gone in having his fun. He's a criminal — an outlaw, plain and outright, and he ain't no different than one of them that holds up a stage or robs a bank, and by Jefferson, he's going to jail for it same as they have to!"

Lingo's jaw tightened and for the first time the sleek assuredness that he wore like a proud crest vanished.

"You'll never get him inside your jail, Sam Culver! I'll see you in hell first!"

The lawman smiled quietly. "Could be we'll all be meeting there, Rufe. Now, get out of here and let me be. Got some business to hash over with my deputy."

The land broker stood motionless for a long breath, eyes sparking angrily, and then abruptly he whirled. With Yancey at his heels, he stalked through the doorway and back into the street.

Culver watched the pair cross to Lingo's office, a faint smile of amusement on his lips, and then glanced to Shawn.

"Well, now, deputy, you've met the old he-coon. Ain't never puzzled it out whether he knows that boy of his is all bad and won't own up to it or whether he's just plain dumb and lets Yancey fool him all the time."

Starbuck shrugged, moved to one of the chairs, and sat down. "Looks to me like he knows he's doing a lot of hellraising but doesn't figure there's anything bad in it."

"Maybe. Could be he ain't going to admit it. Anyway, you see how it is. . . . What was it you wanted to talk about?"

Shawn grinned at the ease with which the old lawman dismissed the Lingo problem. Evidently, while serious, he had lived with it for so long that it was just another chore he would one day complete.

46

"My brother. Been hunting him for quite a spell. Wanted to ask if you'd seen him during your riding around the country."

Culver knitted his brow, tugged at a corner of his beard. "Starbuck," he muttered. "Don't ever recollect hearing the name before."

"Calls himself Damon Friend, I guess. Talked to a man up in Silver City, where Ben —"

"Ben?"

"That's his real name. He put on a boxing match there. Fellow said we looked a lot alike only that Ben was heavier."

The lawman shook his head. "Sure don't think I've ever seen him, or heard the name — either one — before." He hesitated, voiced the usual question. "How's it happen he ain't using his real name? The law after him?"

"No, was a family matter. We lived on a farm back in Ohio. He and my pa had a row over a chore that Ben forgot to take care of. Was a big ruckus and Ben left, saying he'd not come back, ever, and that he was changing his name so's there'd be no family connection."

"I see. And you're out looking for him to take him back."

"Sort of. Pa died and put in his will that I

47

had to find him and bring him to the lawyers before the estate could be settled. Quite a bit of cash involved, besides the fact that I'd like to see him again."

"It been a long time since the row?"

"Around eleven years."

Culver whistled softly. "You mean you've been looking for him that long? Hell, you couldn't've been much more'n a button yourself when —"

"Didn't start right then. I stayed with Pa on the farm — my mother had died a couple of years before Ben left — until his death, then started out. Been just about everywhere. Come close to meeting up with him a few times, like Silver City, but never have made it."

"Expect it's been a mighty hard job. Big country to just go meandering around through looking for a man you don't hardly know. Could spend your life just missing him. . . . You said something about him putting on a boxing match."

"Guess he does that whenever he runs out of cash, or could be that's how he makes a living."

"You do the same? Noticed that fancy belt buckle you're wearing. That mean you're one of them boxers, too, a champion maybe?"

"It belonged to my pa. He was good at it and taught Ben and me. When he died, I claimed it." Shawn looked down at the oblong of engraved silver with the ivory figure of a boxer superimposed upon its surface. "Pa could have been a champion, I expect, but he liked farming and stuck to it."

"Then where'd he get the buckle?"

"He used to put on exhibitions in the town near where we lived. Usually was every weekend. Folks all got together and presented it to him, sort of in appreciation for the shows, I guess."

"Must've been plenty good at it. How about you? You put on these here shows now and then?"

"Nope. When I need cash to travel on, I hunt up a regular job."

"But you said your pa'd taught you —"

"He did. Can take care of myself when I need to."

The lawman grinned. "Sort of got that idea back there in the saloon. . . . Well, I'm plumb sorry I can't help you none about your brother, but I'll start looking and listening a mite closer when I'm out and around. Could be I'll run into him or maybe come across somebody that knows him and can say where he is."

"Man up in Dodge City that runs a sort of

mail service is putting out the word for me. If it's all the same to you I'll drop him a letter, tell him he can reach me here at your office for the next few months — if he needs to."

"That's the thing to do. Right now, you better get your gear and tote it down to your cabin. Where's your horse?"

"Stabled him at Feather's livery barn."

"Ike's place is as good as any. Been aiming to put up a shed here but just ain't got around to it yet."

Starbuck got to his feet, started for the door, halted. "Anything special about this deputy job that I ought to know?"

Culver looked up from the papers he was taking out of the desk, a frown on his face. "Special? Hell, no. I ain't beholden to no man. Anybody breaking the law gets jugged — and you've been around enough to know when that's getting done. Why? You maybe got an idea that I shut my eyes to —"

"Just wanted to be sure of my ground."

"You can be plenty sure. Far as I'm concerned everybody looks alike."

"That makes it easy," Starbuck said and stepped out into the closing night.

6

The deputy sheriff's star pinned to his shirt drew immediate attention, Starbuck noted, as he bent his steps toward the Wagonwheel Saloon. Some of the people along the street frowned as if disapproving, others merely stared, concealing whatever reaction overtook them. He was undisturbed; there was no good reason that he could see why he should not accept the commission — and Sam Culver certainly could use help.

He slowed, catching sight of Sarah York standing alone in front of Dolan's General Store. Changing course, he angled across the roadway, and pulling off his hat, halted before her.

"Was hoping I'd get a moment to talk to you —"

She considered him gravely. The fading, mellow light enhanced the cameolike beauty of her features and darkened the blue of her eyes.

"I — I don't know," she said hesitantly. "I'm waiting for my father. If he should see us —"

"This won't take long. Just like for you to

know that I'm no hired killer. I don't go around shooting men because I like it. If I hadn't used my gun when I did the sheriff would be dead."

She moved her head slightly. "Papa doesn't approve of a man killing another for any reason."

"There are times when it can't be helped. I'm not proud of it but I'm not ashamed of it either. Happens I'm a man like most others, making a living at cowpunching, trail driving, and jobs like that."

"And being a deputy sheriff," Sarah added, looking at his badge.

"That, too. This is not the first time I've worn a star. Far as I'm concerned a job's a job, something I can make a little money at so's I can keep moving."

"Moving — a drifter!" There was a trace of regret in her voice.

"Maybe. Fact is I'm hunting for my brother. Once I find him things will change. Hope to settle down then."

She nodded slowly. "I guess I understand — but Papa never would. He says you're an instrument of the Devil — a lost soul who has traded all your tomorrows for today."

Shawn grinned. "He's a great one with words, but he's hanging the wrong tag on me."

The girl returned his smile. She glanced away, turning her even, near-perfect profile to him. "I'm glad," she murmured almost inaudibly.

"This is a good town," he said then, also glancing around. "Think I'll like working here — like it a lot better, though, if I could call on you sometime."

"You know the answer to that," Sarah said quickly. "Papa wouldn't hear of it."

"That wouldn't bother me any. Be up to you."

"Perhaps, but I couldn't go against his wishes — not that I wouldn't like for you to."

She had colored slightly at the boldness of her words. Starbuck nodded. "If you're agreeable that's all I need. I'll see the reverend, have a talk with him, and try to change his ideas about me."

"He won't change — especially now that you've gone to work for Sheriff Culver."

Starbuck was silent for a moment. Along the street were the hushed sounds of the day's end — the contented chirping of birds in the trees, the quiet, gentle noises of people preparing for the night, the weary shuffling about of horses in a nearby stable. Somewhere beyond the edge of the settlement a cow lowed forlornly.

"That because of the trouble between

Culver and Rufus Lingo?"

"Mostly. He feels that the sheriff has something personal against him and is taking it out on Yancey."

"What do you think?"

Sarah's small shoulders twitched. "Oh, I don't know. I try not to think about such things. I can never discuss them with Papa. He always makes me see that he's right and I'm wrong, no matter what, so to keep peace, I avoid arguing."

"Well, I'm new around here and my mind's not made up about folks, but from what I've seen so far the sheriff's right. Everything happened just the way he said it did in the saloon — and Yancey is a bad one. One of these days he's going to get himself into the kind of trouble that he can't climb out of."

"What about Mr. Lingo?"

"No judge of him. Figures himself plenty big and powerful, I can see that, but that's not unusual. Most men, once they get rich, start feeling that way. Could be he really believes Yancey's all right and that Sam Culver's just making it hard on him."

"Then Papa could be right."

"Not about Yancey. Sheriff has some things on him that could put him behind bars. All he's holding back for is proof."

Sarah stirred tiredly. "I hope he never gets

it. Not that Yancey Lingo means anything to me — I hardly know him — but for Papa."

"I've heard Rufus Lingo's friendship means a lot to him."

"It does, and for only one reason — the church. He's worked so hard to bring God into Kennesaw and he's been able to do it only because of Mr. Lingo's help. If anything happens to him —"

"Seems to me the reverend is depending on the wrong party," Starbuck said drily. "God can take care of His own without somebody like Lingo."

Lamplight was showing now in several store windows along the street. Sarah contemplated the soft glow, smiled wearily. "There have been times when I wondered if God was on Papa's side. . . . There's something I've wanted to ask," she added as if anxious to change the subject. "Was one of your parents Indian? The name Shawn —"

"No, but my mother worked among the Shawnee tribe. She was a schoolteacher. Liked the sound of the word, I guess, and when I came along she made it into a name for me."

"Were you born in the Indian Territory?"

"No, Ohio. Folks had a farm there. They're both dead now, and the place has been sold."

"I see. I wondered about you, thought that

you'd probably been brought up somewhere back East and had had some schooling. Out here things like that show up."

"Expect you came from some other part of the country, too."

"Boston — oh, here comes papa. You'd better go. I'd hate for there to be a scene."

Starbuck nodded. "Sure, long as you say I can see you again."

"If we get the chance," she replied hurriedly.

He replaced his hat, touched its brim, and turned away, pointing for the Wagonwheel Saloon. Off to the left he could see Ahab York moving toward him in long, stiff-kneed strides, head erect, body rigid and unyielding.

"Starbuck!"

At the sharp call Shawn stopped, faced about.

"Saw you talking to my daughter! I'll not have that — understand! I don't want you near her!"

York's voice trembled with anger. It was not the moment for a rational discussion. Shawn smiled, nodded, and moved on, giving the man no reply. He reached the steps of the Wagonwheel, mounted and crossed the porch to the swinging doors. As he entered, he looked over his shoulder. The tall minister was standing beside his daughter, speaking with considerable agitation and vehemence.

Undoubtedly Sarah was being served the same ultimatum that had been accorded him. Would she accept it meekly, or would she find somewhere within herself a spark of rebellion and independence? He wondered.

Stepping into the saloon, he paused to let his eyes sweep the room, saw Nella rise from a table near the end of the bar. A puzzled expression crossed her face as she noted the star he was wearing. By the time they had met, near center of the area, a smile had wiped away the frown.

"You're staying —"

"For a while," he answered. "Came after my gear. A shack goes with the job."

"Why not just stay here?"

"Shack'll be handier," he said, and nodded to Whitcomb, who was also registering surprise.

Moving on past the girl, he climbed to the second floor. Making his way to the quarters he'd been occupying, he collected his gear, and hanging it over a shoulder, returned to ground level. Whitcomb was waiting for him.

"When'd all this happen?"

"Little bit ago. Was looking for a job, found one."

"I don't see why you can't keep on living

here," Nella said petulantly.

"Wouldn't look right," Whitcomb explained. "Lawman can't be rooming over a saloon. . . . Glad to see old Sam's got himself some help."

"He needs it," the girl said. "Sure was a good thing you were around when that ruckus with Yancey started. We'd be needing a sheriff instead of a deputy."

"Never mind Yancey," the saloon man said cautiously.

Nella tossed her head. "Never have — him or his pa either, and they don't scare me none."

"Maybe not, but you'd best keep your lip buttoned about them if you aim to keep on working here," Whitcomb snapped and moved on down the counter to serve an impatient customer.

Starbuck pulled away. Nella caught him by the arm. "I'm glad you're not leaving — but I wonder if it was smart to take the job?"

"Why not? One's about as good as another."

"I know, but with everybody feeling the way they do about Sam Culver —"

Nella's words broke off as a muffled gunshot echoed through the darkness along the street. Wheeling, Starbuck crossed hurriedly to the doorway.

7

Two men were standing on the Wagon-wheel's porch looking down the barely lit roadway. Elsewhere along the sidewalks others were appearing, coming from their homes or shops, pausing, glancing about questioningly.

"Where'd that shot come from?" Starbuck asked, halting beside the pair.

"Down that way," one replied, pointing. "Somewheres near the jail, seemed."

Alarm lifted within Shawn. Pushing past the patrons of the saloon, now following him through the swinging doors, he stepped off the broad landing, at once shifting the saddlebags and blanket roll he was carrying to his right arm in order to free the left. Avoiding the thump of his boot heel striking on the dry boards of the walk by staying in the loose dust, he hurried past the buildings. Halfway to the sheriff's quarters he slowed, arrested by vague motion at the extreme lower end of the street.

Whatever or whoever it was vanished almost instantly, affording him but a glimpse, and he pressed on at an urgent pace, the alarm he had felt earlier steadily increasing. He tried to allay his fears, telling himself that it could have been only the accidental discharging of a weapon, or a man shooting at a prowling coyote, even a cowboy with a bit too much to drink whooping it up in one of the saloons, but none of the possible explanations satisfied him.

Tense, he drew near the corner of the jail, swung toward the oblong of lamplight spilling through the doorway into the night. He halted, an oath breaking from his lips.

Sprawled on the floor was Sam Culver. He lay face down, arms extended beyond his head, a pool of blood seeping out from under his chest.

Starbuck flung his gear onto a nearby chair, dropped to the lawman's side. On down the narrow corridor that ran by the cells he could see an open door — the exit used by whoever had shot down Culver, he supposed.

Thrusting his fingers into the lawman's neck, Shawn searched for a pulse. There was none. He settled back on his heels, remembering the dark blur of motion in the shadows. The killer — or killers, no doubt — probably after entering and leaving by the rear door of the jail had taken that route in a hasty flight.

Starbuck frowned, his eyes fixing upon markings in the dust near Culver's out-stretched hand. He leaned forward, looked more closely. Two lines, faint and unsteady, one intersecting the other around midway. Next to those another mark. He studied them thoughtfully. Was the first figure meant to be a *Y,* the following the start of a second letter — an *A* possibly? Had Sam Culver been trying to name his killer before death overtook him? If so the word he was attempting to spell could only be *YANCEY.*

Starbuck's features hardened as that real-ization came to him, but he had to be sure. Aware now of boots pounding in the street outside the jail as men hurried up, he rose, moved around to where he could reach the lawman's outstretched arm. Taking up the spread hand, he examined the forefinger carefully. The tip was smudged with dust, all others were clean. There was no doubt Culver had been leaving a message when he died.

"It's Sam — is he dead?"

Shawn lowered the lawman's hand to the floor, came upright, and faced the doorway. A half-dozen or more men were gathered in and around the opening.

"The sheriff's been murdered," he re-plied.

61

Someone swore deeply. Another said, "Better go get Dolan and Matt Rittenhouse. The reverend, too, I expect. And Doc Grey."

"Dolan's coming now."

The crowd parted. Dolan, a tall, blond man with sharp brown eyes, stepped into the room. He halted abruptly when he saw Culver's prone shape.

"What —"

"He's been murdered," Starbuck repeated and pointed to the faint scrawling in the dust. "Looks like he tried to spell out the name of the killer. Made a *Y* and started the next letter — an *A,* I figure. Died before he could finish."

The general store owner crouched over the marks, nodded slowly. "Something there, all right."

"Way I see it he was trying to spell out 'Yancey.'" Dolan got to his feet, eyes snapping. "Yancey! You claiming Yancey Lingo shot him?"

The merchant's disbelief and hostility brought a flood of anger to Starbuck. "There anybody else around here whose name starts with a *Y* and that's been having trouble with the sheriff?"

The crowd, growing larger as word of the killing sped along the street, parted, this time to admit York and a small, dark man that Starbuck had heard was the town banker, Matt Rittenhouse.

Ahab York's features were taut and gray as he looked down at the lawman. Rittenhouse shook his head sorrowfully and glanced at Shawn. A flicker of surprise showed in his eyes as he noticed the star but he made no comment, said instead: "Who did it? Any idea?"

"Yancey Lingo, according to him," Dolan supplied and pointed to the marks in the dust. "Claims Sam was trying to write out Yancey's name before he croaked."

York circled the body, bent forward to have his look at the lines. He drew up skeptically.

"Doubt that," he said in a firm voice. "Man in pain would be clawing, working his fingers. That's why he made those marks." Turning his gaze to Starbuck, he added, "That all you got to base your accusation on?"

"It's enough," Shawn replied, evenly.

"Could've been somebody grudging Sam," one of the men near the door said. "Drifter, maybe."

"Where were you when it happened, Deputy?" Rittenhouse asked.

"At the Wagonwheel picking up my gear.

Heard the shot and came straight here."

"You didn't see anybody leaving?"

"Was somebody crossing the street below. Too dark to tell who it was."

"Probably the killer," Dolan said, "and more'n likely somebody from out in the county that had it in for Sam."

"I'll stay with Yancey Lingo," Shawn said quietly. "He had a reason — and those aren't just scratches in the dust. The sheriff was naming his killer. Take a look at the rest of his fingers. Dust on one, none on the others. If he'd been clawing, they would have all been covered."

Dolan squatted beside the lawman's body again, and lifting the stiffening arm, studied the fingertips of the hand. "He's right. Dirt's only on one."

A murmur ran through the crowd. York shook his head. "Don't jump to conclusions. I don't think the son of Rufus Lingo would stoop to murder. Besides, we all know the sheriff bore nothing but bad feeling for the boy."

"You mean he could've done that scratching of Yancey's name just for spite?" a voice wondered.

York glanced around. "I will not speak ill of the dead, but such seems likely to me."

"Now, wait a minute, Reverend,"

Rittenhouse said. "You're the one jumping to conclusions. Has anybody seen Yancey around since this afternoon?"

There was a brief silence and then a slim-faced man outside the office on the landing said, "I sure ain't, an he gen'rly comes by my place. Horse is gone. Was standing out in front of his pa's along with two, three others. Ain't none of them there now."

"Lingo's office is dark, too."

Rittenhouse came back to Starbuck. "Those men — if that's what you saw at the end of the street — you couldn't tell who they were?"

"Too dark."

"How many of them?"

"Couldn't be sure of that, either. More than one — if what I saw was men."

The banker shrugged. "No help there. Might have been a horse or it could have been somebody in town going to visit a neighbor —"

"But most likely it was the sheriff's killer — and far as I'm concerned that's Yancey Lingo. Probably had his two friends with him."

"Billy Joe and Red Davis?"

Shawn nodded. "I'll arrest the three of them, bring them in for trial. That writing in the dust is all I need. A jury can decide

65

whether they're guilty or not."

"Sounds fair enough to me," Rittenhouse said.

"Not to me!" York boomed. "It's wrong to even accuse the boy and his friends on such evidence! For all we know the deputy there could have made those marks himself!"

"That's right!" a man in the forefront of the crowd declared. "He was holding Sam's hand in his when we got here. Could be he took the sheriff's finger and made them letters so's there'd be dust on it."

8

Rufus Lingo was sitting alone in the small study he had arranged in the rear of his office when the flat, hollow echo of the gunshot marking the death of Sam Culver reached him. He had not as yet lit one of the several lamps in the room but was simply taking his ease, enjoying the quiet and the dark.

The quick snap of the weapon caught at his attention, and he paused to consider it. The sound had come from the street — and nearby, he thought. It was a bit unusual; there had been no shootings in Kennesaw for some time, up until that very afternoon, in fact, when Culver's new deputy had shot down Harley Greer. Now, here was a second; Kennesaw appeared to be returning to the old days when gunfights were a daily occurrence.

He could hear shouting. Rising, Lingo crossed to the opening that let into the main part of the office and glanced through the window into the street. A scatter of men were running toward the sheriff's office. Inside it he could see the shadow of someone standing near a wall, but it was not possible to tell who that person was.

A key clicked in the outer door of the study. Frowning, he wheeled as the panel swung open. A match flared, died instantly as Yancey's impatient voice reached him.

"Don't strike no light, dammit! Somebody might see it."

Lingo stepped back into the study, closing the inner door behind him. At once Yancey said, "Pa?"

"Right here. What's the trouble? Why not light a lamp?"

There was a moment's hesitation on the younger man's part, and then, "Just don't want nobody knowing I'm — we're here."

"Who's with you?"

"Billy Joe and Red."

"Thought you were all going out to the ranch?"

"Was," Yancey replied, and moved deeper into the room. In the pale moonlight stealing through a lone window set high in the wall his eyes were bright, hard. "Had a little business we had to take care of."

"That so?" Lingo said cautiously.

"Yeh. . . . Pa, you don't have to worry none about Sam Culver no more. He's dead."

Rufus Lingo stiffened and a dryness filled his throat. "Lock that door," he murmured, and crossing the room, drew the thick roller shade over the window pane. Turning back to his desk, he fired a match, and lifting the glass chimney, held it to the lamp's wick until the tiny flame caught. Resetting the cylinder, he came about slowly, almost reluctantly, and faced his son.

"How do you know Culver's dead?" he asked in a tight voice.

"Was me that shot him," Yancey said blandly.

Lingo's shoulders sagged. "You — you killed him?"

"Me and Billy Joe and Red. We was together. I done the shooting."

A strangled sound escaped the older man's throat. "Why — in God's name — why?"

Yancey shrugged, settled himself on a corner of the desk. "He's been riding me hard — and I don't take that from nobody. Was doing it for you, too. Heard you say many a time you wished to hell you could get shut of him."

"Not that way," Lingo groaned despairingly.

Long ago he had given up trying to understand his son. He had failed completely in the hope of raising him in his own likeness, even where schooling was concerned.

69

Yancey had simply been unable to learn, either by choice or because of a fault in his mental makeup. In all other endeavors his efforts had gone for naught, also. Perhaps he might have turned out different if his mother had lived, but passing away while the boy was still only an infant —

There was nothing to be gained by hashing that over, however; what was done was done, and steps must be taken to remedy the situation. He could no more afford to let it be known that the son of Rufus Lingo was a murderer than he could let that son go to the gallows.

"Anybody see you?"

Yancey shook his head. "Wasn't nobody around. We snuck in the jail by the back way. The sheriff was setting at his desk writing something. I told him plain out I was tired of him crawling me all the time and then when he got up, I plugged him good. We went out the back same as we went in and then come here. . . . Place being all dark I figured you was gone to the house or maybe the ranch."

"You sure nobody saw you on your way here?"

"Plenty sure. We seen somebody running in the street — that goddam drifter that shot Harley, I reckon it was, but he couldn't've seen us. Was dark and we was clean down at the end of town."

"Expect he saw you, all right, but chances are he couldn't recognize you."

Lingo paused, considered his next move. Now that the initial shock of what Yancey had done was past, it was necessary he think clearly, determine what was best for him and his interests — and, of course, for Yancey. It was unfortunate there had been witnesses to the killing.

The fact that Spicer and Davis were friends of the boy meant nothing. Both would undoubtedly talk up, tell everything they knew, if caught by the law and given to understand their own lives were at stake unless the truth was forthcoming. Yancey had a knack for choosing the sort of companions that had no conception of loyalty.

Abruptly the land broker came to a decision. The wise thing was to get all three of them out of sight — out of town, make it appear they had been gone since the middle of the afternoon and therefore not around when the killing took place. He leaned forward in his chair.

"Best thing now is for you to leave here — right away."

Yancey's head came up. He glanced at Billy Joe and Davis, frowned. "Why, Pa?

Nobody seen us, and there ain't no reason for somebody to think I done it."

"You don't know for certain that you weren't spotted going in and out of the jail — or crossing the street. You only think so. And all hell's going to break loose. You don't seem to realize what you've done! Wasn't only Sam Culver you killed, but it was a lawman, and that means trouble. Like as not we'll have the U.S. marshal down here as soon as he knows about it. That deputy, Starbuck or whatever his name is, he won't let it pass, either."

"Just let him try pinning it on me and I'll —"

Rufus Lingo came to his feet. "You'll do exactly what I tell you to!" he snapped. "I mean all three of you. You're all in it, and if anything goes wrong they'll hang the lot of you, so you had better listen close to what I have to say.

"We've got to make it look like you left town early — long before the killing happened. I'll put out the word that you went off somewhere to get drunk, that you were feeling bad about Greer getting shot —"

"Could go to the ranch."

"Too risky. One of the hands might say he hadn't seen you around, and we'd be fools to take the whole crew in on it. Best we let them think like the rest of the town — that you're off on a toot. Anybody asks me just where you went I'll say I don't know."

Billy Joe stirred nervously. "Where you reckon we could hide then, Mr. Lingo? I sure don't want to get myself tangled up with the law."

"You already are," the older man said harshly. "You and Red are in it deep as Yancey. Means you've got to stay together, look out for each other."

Davis hawked, spat into the brass cuspidor at the end of the desk. "That maybe ain't so," he said. "We tried talking Yancey out of doing it, but he wouldn't listen. Told him myself it was a dumb fool thing to do."

"You should have made him listen," the land broker snapped. "Way it is now you're guilty as he is. Nobody will ever believe you tried to stop it." He started to add that he, personally, would see to that point, but let it ride. It was a threat he could use later if it became necessary to keep the two men in line.

The redhead shrugged. "Well, where you wanting us to go?"

Lingo thought for a moment. "How about that old mine shack up on Cougar Mesa? Understand you've spent some time there before — you and some lady friends."

Yancey and the others exchanged glances. "How'd you know that?" he asked.

Rufus Lingo permitted himself a brief, dry smile. "Women talk — especially the kind you drag up there for your weekend brawls. Being on ranch property it'll be about the safest place you can lay out in. You're not apt to see anybody unless it's one of the hired hands looking for strays. If that happens you're up there drowning your grief for Greer with whiskey. Understand?"

Yancey nodded vaguely, said, "Sure. How long you want us to stay?"

"Four or five days at least. I'll come myself when things've quieted down."

"But just supposing one of them cowpunchers comes by —"

"Won't make any difference once you're there. Story I'll put out is that you headed out this afternoon — I've already explained that to you! See that you tell the same thing — you weren't in town at the time Culver was killed, so it couldn't have been any of you that did it. Have you got it straight now?"

"Sure, but it won't be no chore keeping somebody from coming up there. Only one trail and we can keep watching it."

"Forget it!" Lingo said quickly. "You use a gun to keep somebody away and they'll

74

know something's wrong. Get it into your head — you feel bad about Harley Greer, you're off getting drunk so's you can forget it."

"I savvy, Pa."

Davis spat again into the cuspidor. "That go for the new deputy, too?"

The older man gave that thought. There was something about Starbuck that turned him uneasy, a quiet deadliness of purpose in his manner that bespoke an unwavering determination. Allowing him to get with Yancey and the others, press them with questions, could be a fatal mistake.

"He's the exception. He shows up, let him make it to the top, then get rid of him — and bury him deep so he'll never be found."

"You mean we should kill him?" Billy Joe said in a high, strained voice.

"You've already got one murder to your credit. Another one covering it up won't make any difference. They can only hang you once." Lingo turned his head toward the street. The crowd was still there, gathered in front of the sheriff's office, he guessed. He could hear a voice now and then. It would be smart to put in an appearance — and he could if he hurried.

"Everything straight?"

"Reckon so. What'll we do for grub, Pa?

75

Place was stripped pretty clean last time we was up there."

The land broker reached into his pocket, produced two double eagles. "Buy some. Ride over to Carrsville and stock up there," he said, handing the coins to Yancey. "Can't afford to be seen around here. . . . Where's your horses?"

"Old shed out in back of Merino's."

"Good. Get them quick and move on. Swing east, away from town, so's you won't be seen — and don't show up here again. I'll come for you when it's safe."

"All right," Yancey said and drew himself off the desk.

Lingo turned to the lamp, twisted down its wick. With the room filled with darkness, he crossed to the door, unlocked and opened it.

"Be careful," he murmured as the three men passed by and entered the alley.

Red Davis caught at Yancey's arm as, in single file, they moved off into the night.

"Best we keep close to the buildings in the shadows. Like your pa said, we don't want anybody seeing us."

Yancey jerked away impatiently. "Goddammit, I heard him!"

They hurried on, came to the shelter

where their horses were tied. Lingo wheeled to Davis, handed him one of the double eagles.

"We're doing this my way from here on. Now, soon's we're out of town, you light out for Carrsville and get us a few quarts of liquor. We ain't spending none of this money for grub — not while Billy Joe and me can go by the ranch and pick us up all we need from the cook. . . . We'll meet you later at the shack."

Davis hesitated briefly, and then pocketing the coin, turned to his horse. In the saddle he paused again as Yancey caught at his bridle.

"Something else. Why'n't you scare us up a gal apiece so's we'll have company to do our sorrowing with. Going to get mighty lonesome up there — just us."

Red Davis nodded, said, "For a fact," and rode on.

9

Starbuck surveyed the crowd coldly, shrugged. "Was looking to see if the sheriff made those marks intentionally. Dust on just one finger proved he did."

"Not to me," York said stubbornly. "I think Joe has a point — you could have used the sheriff's finger to —"

"Can't see as he'd have a reason to," Rittenhouse broke in. "Wasn't any trouble between him and Yancey, and he hasn't been around long enough to take sides in the town's squabbles."

There was a commotion at the entrance to the office. Shortly a squat, elderly man with a scarred medical bag pushed through the closely packed bystanders. He glanced around, knelt beside the body of the lawman, made a quick examination.

"Dead, of course," he said, rising. "One bullet, close range. Right into the heart, it appears. . . . Know who did it?" he added, fixing his eyes on Shawn.

Starbuck pointed to the lines on the floor. The physician crouched again, studied the marks. "Looks like a *Y* and the beginning of another letter."

"The deputy figures it's an *A*," Dolan said. "Claims it stands for Yancey — that the sheriff was trying to tell who killed him. Died before he could finish."

"Sounds reasonable," the doctor said, checking the tips of Culver's fingers. "In fact, I'd say he was right."

"And I say he's wrong!" Ahab York boomed. "It's only a guess — and a bad one. Marks could have been there, or, like Joe Harris says, the deputy might have made them himself so's to blame the murder on Yancey Lingo."

Doc Grey looked around blankly. "Now, why would he do that?"

"To get back at Yancey — or maybe he wants to be sheriff, since he's right in line for the job now that Sam Culver's dead. Finding the murderer quick would make him look real good."

"Oh, fiddlesticks!" the medical man said in disgust.

"Doubt if he could care less about being sheriff — and far as getting back at Yancey Lingo, if you're going to use that as a reason, Reverend, you'll have to ring in half the county's population. . . . Couple of you men pick up the sheriff and carry him over to Henry's for me. Might as well get him

79

ready for burying. Can lay him and Greer away at the same time."

Grey turned as several onlookers stepped forward, took up the body of the old lawman between them. The doorway cleared long enough for them to pass through and quickly closed again.

In the silence that followed, Starbuck moved in behind the desk. He swept the gathering with a glance, said, "Show's over. Like for you to clear out, let me get on about my business."

No one stirred. He was a comparative stranger in their midst, suddenly thrust into prominence, and he could feel the mistrust and resentment they held for him. Dolan voiced it.

"What do you think you're going to do?"

"Arrest Yancey Lingo for murder."

"You can't!" Ahab York shouted, shaking his finger at Shawn. "You don't have the right."

"Back off, Reverend," Rittenhouse said calmly. "The deputy's the law here now, and he figures he has good reason to suspect Yancey. Frankly, so do I."

"Well, I don't," Dolan said flatly. "And far as him being in charge around here, we can plenty quick change that."

"I'm not so sure," the banker said.

80

"Starbuck's been legally sworn in, and it could be there's nothing the town can do about it. If you're set on trying to block him, however, the thing to do is get the council together and talk about it."

"Just what I aim to do," the merchant said, voice tight with anger. "Meantime, Deputy, you just let things ride."

"Not about to," Starbuck replied. "My duty to bring the man in, hold him for trial."

"And maybe be forced to shoot him like you had to do Harley Greer," York said scornfully.

"Up to him. . . . Asked you once to clear out — I'm telling you now."

"He's right," Rittenhouse said, turning and moving toward the door. "We're interfering with a man trying to do his job — as he sees it."

The crowd gave way before him, began to pass through the opening reluctantly, came to a halt in the street. Dolan, accompanied by York, hurried off at once, however, doubtless to round up the remaining members of the town council so that a meeting designed to relieve him of his authority could be held.

Starbuck watched them go thoughtfully. He had no illusions with regards to his position; excepting banker Rittenhouse and

Doc Grey, the entire town was against him where Yancey Lingo was concerned — and for the simple reason that Yancey was the son of Rufus Lingo and not because he could be innocent of murder.

None of it mattered. He would perform the task he'd sworn to do, that of upholding the law, and if the town fathers saw fit to step in and remove his badge, he'd go ahead anyway; he owed that much to Sam Culver — and to the law itself.

The office was warm and silent now that it had emptied. Pausing to check the pistol on his hip and finding it ready, he crossed to the doorway and stepped out onto the landing. The majority of the crowd was still there, assembled in the center of the street, sullenly watching and waiting. On the opposite sidewalk, a short distance away, he saw Sarah York standing with two older women. He wondered what her thoughts were regarding him and the matter of Yancey Lingo, guessed they would likely coincide with those of her father.

Shrugging, he dismissed her from his mind, glanced to Lingo's office. It lay in darkness, and as someone had noted earlier, the horses that had been at its hitchrack were gone. Leaving the landing, he stalked past the crowd, tense, eyes straight ahead, and pointed for the land broker's building. Reaching it, he stopped at its entrance, tried the knob. It was locked.

"They ain't there — ain't been there all afternoon," a man in the crowd said, a note of derision in his voice. "You been told that."

"You're barking up the wrong tree, Deputy," another added.

Shawn gave no sign of having heard. Doubling back across the front of the structure, he turned into the darkness laying along its north wall, and aware of the crowd following a short distance at his heels, made his way to the rear. There were two doors — both also locked. He started to wheel, checked as a figure emerged from the shadows on the far side of the alley.

"There something I can do for you?"

A moment later Starbuck recognized Rufus Lingo, but before he could answer the man called Joe Harris spoke up.

"He's looking for Yancey. Claims he killed the sheriff."

Lingo moved into the faint light seeping from the window of an adjacent building. Amazement covered his features. "Culver? He's been murdered?"

"About an hour ago," Shawn said, studying the man narrowly. "You saying you didn't hear the shot? Was right across the street."

The land broker frowned. "Yes, I guess I did. Went for a stroll after it got dark — toward the river. Remember now I did hear a noise — a report. It could have been a gunshot. . . . But what's my son got to do with it?"

"The sheriff scratched, or started to scratch, Yancey's name in the dust on the floor before he died. Was naming his killer. I'm arresting him and holding him for trial."

Lingo shook his head. "I'm afraid you're wrong, Deputy. You say it happened an hour or so ago? Yancey's been gone since the middle of the afternoon."

"Gone? Where?"

"I don't exactly know. He felt mighty bad about Harley Greer's death. So did Billy Joe and Red Davis. Told me they were going to take a little ride and try and forget about it. A little ride to them means going off to some other town and holing up with a few quarts of whiskey." Lingo looked around the crowd, smiled. "You all know how boys are."

Starbuck's steady gaze did not waver. "I saw somebody cross the street right after it happened —"

The probing statement failed. Rufus

Lingo shrugged. "Couldn't have been Yancey. He's been gone for hours, like I said. Afraid you're mistaken if you think it was him. Did you get a good look?"

"No, was too dark, and too far."

"Then all you're going on are those marks you found on the floor."

"And we think maybe he done that hisself," Harris said. "The Reverend thinks so, too."

Lingo stroked his chin. "Hardly can believe that, Joe, but I guess it could be true. Can't see as he'd have anything to gain —"

"Wants to make a name for hisself so's he can get the sheriff's job," Harris said firmly.

The land broker's brows lifted. "Hadn't thought of that!" he said in a surprised tone. "But no matter, he's wrong. Yancey couldn't have done it. The same goes for Red and Billy Joe. They weren't in town."

Starbuck smiled grimly. There was no point in wasting further time with Rufus Lingo.

"Maybe — far as you know," he said, and wheeling, cut back through the crowd for the jail.

10

Reaching the street, Shawn turned his glance to where he had earlier noticed Sarah. She was no longer there, and what few persons were in sight had gathered in front of the undertaking parlor.

Crossing over, he entered the jail, his thoughts again on Yancey and on Rufus Lingo as well. There was no lessening of the conviction in his mind that the younger Lingo was the killer of Sam Culver — and he wasn't too certain that the older member of the family was not aware of it. The land broker's answers were all too pat, too readily available, and what seemed strange to Starbuck was that the man appeared hardly disturbed by the accusation.

Rufus, according to the sheriff, was a smooth one, but it was only logical to believe that a father hearing of his son being sought for murder would display at least a small amount of alarm and concern. Instead he had blandly and efficiently fielded the questions put to him regarding Yancey much as he might have had he been in a courtroom explaining a business deal. It was almost as if he had come prepared for the confrontation.

Standing there in the center of the littered office, Shawn considered his situation, a tall, well-built man in his early twenties with deep-set eyes and a square, blocky face that gave him the appearance of being much older than he actually was. Pulling off his hat, he ran a hand through his dark hair and then mopped at the sweat on his forehead with the back of a wrist.

He hadn't bargained for this sort of thing when he allowed Sam Culver to swear him in as a deputy, and he vaguely wished now that he had followed his original plan to ride on, find himself a job on some ranch where all he needed to worry about were strays, prowling wolves and coyotes, and maybe a rustler or two.

He'd done a time now and then as a lawman, keeping the peace, and had no taste for the quite frequent conclusion where the use of the gun slung low on his left leg became necessary. Killing a man, regardless of the crime committed, was never a moment of glory for him and usually stuck in his mind for days to come.

But there was no turning away from responsibility now. He was saddled with the chore, and he'd not let down until it was completed. Yancey Lingo was the killer, the man he wanted, and no amount of talk from anyone would convince him otherwise. Thus the matter at hand was to find him, bring him in.

Moving to the doorway, he stepped out again into the street. Night was a disadvantage, making more difficult the job that lay before him, but it would be unwise to wait for morning, since the odds were about even that Yancey and the pair that sided him were still somewhere in town.

Angling right, Shawn walked to the lower end of the now wholly deserted street to that point where he had seen someone crossing. There was no way of being certain it had been Yancey and his friends, he knew — but somebody had passed that way, for certain. Further, they had appeared shortly after the gunshot was heard, and had been heading for the side of the street on which Rufus Lingo's office stood.

All of which could mean nothing, he admitted as he looked thoughtfully about. It was too dark to tell anything from tracks, and even in daylight about all that might be determined was the number of persons in the party.

Continuing on the same course taken by whoever it had been, Shawn passed along the side of the building gracing the corner and reached the alley that lay behind it and other structures on that side of the roadway. Veering into it, he strode quietly along the dark lane, noting the rears of the buildings, the periodic sheds and lean-to shelters used by the occupants for their horses.

Abreast the back entrance of Lingo's office he paused for a few moments to listen. All was silent and utterly black beyond the solitary, shaded window in the wall. Evidently the land broker had locked up for the night and gone to his home.

Resuming the patrol, Shawn came to the vacant lot that lay this side of the undertaker's quarters and there cut back to the street. He should have a look behind the buildings in the opposite row, see if there were any horses waiting in the dark, or perhaps come upon someone, a drifter possibly, or a cowhand sleeping off a drunk, who might have seen three riders.

But that would come later. Wading through the loose dust, he headed for the Wagonwheel Saloon, mounted the steps to its porch, and entered. The crowd was large, made so by the death of Sam Culver and a desire among the men of the town to talk of it — and probably of him and his declaration to bring in Yancey Lingo for the lawman's murder despite opposition.

Considering such, he had little hope of getting any helpful information, but experience had taught him never to take such things for granted. Smiling at Nella, who arose from a table where she was sitting with two city-dressed men, he made his way to the bar. The steady din was such that it overrode all else, and nodding to Pete Whitcomb in preliminary apology, he drew his pistol and fired a shot into the floor.

As the hubbub died in the resounding echoes and drifting layers of smoke, Starbuck faced the startled patrons in the room.

"I'm looking for Yancey Lingo. Want him for the murder of Sheriff Culver. If any of you know where he is, it's your duty to speak up."

Most of those in the Wagonwheel would have been members of the crowd that had earlier hung around the jail and later trailed him to Lingo's office. He could expect no help from them, and that fact made itself evident immediately.

"You know damned well he ain't around here!" a man at the end of the counter said. "His pa told you he'd gone — and when."

"Got only his word on that," Shawn replied. "If any of you saw Yancey and those two that run with him leave, I'd like to hear about it."

There was no response. "How about horses? Any of you see three horses tied up anywhere around in that end of town?"

Only silence. Starbuck shrugged. "Obliged to you," he said, his voice carrying an edge of scorn. "Sam Culver was your friend, whether you ever admitted it to yourself or not. I reckon you'd like to help catch his murderer if you could."

Abruptly he wheeled about, faced Whitcomb. "I can use a drink — rye."

The saloon man reached for a shot glass, filled it from a half-empty bottle as the drone of conversations began to rise again. He leaned forward.

"You dead set on it being Yancey that done it?"

"No doubt, far as I'm concerned."

Whitcomb waited while Starbuck downed his whiskey, then said, "Well, if it is I expect you'll have to run him down alone. Ain't nobody around here going to give you a hand."

"Figured that out back at the jail but I was working on the hope there'd maybe be one man not afraid of Rufus Lingo — or beholden to him."

"The weight's all on his side. Clem Dolan

and Dave Bristow — he runs the hotel — were in here a spell back. They're rounding up the town council. Aim to fire you."

"Heard that earlier, too. Won't do them any good. They take my badge I'll go right ahead anyway. Sam Culver represented the law. Not right to let the man who killed him get by with it just because his pa's a big man."

"But if you ain't no deputy —"

"They haven't taken my star yet, and if they do I'm not sure they can make it stick. Rittenhouse mentioned it, and it set me to thinking. The sheriff was responsible to the whole county, not just to this town. Expect the same applies to his deputy. I don't know what the legal rigmarole is but I doubt if a town council can get rid of a deputy since he works for the county, not them."

Whitcomb's heavy features showed surprise. "By hell, I never thought of that — and I'll bet Dolan and the others ain't either!"

Nella moved in beside Shawn. He glanced at her, motioned to Whitcomb to pour her a drink. She smiled, took up the glass, and studied him over its rim. Someone down the counter pounded for attention, and the saloon man moved off hurriedly.

"Hoping I can count on you for some help," Shawn said. "If you hear anything —"

"For old time's sake," she cut in, and downed the liquor.

"For that and because Yancey shouldn't be running loose. He'll kill somebody else now that he's found out how easy it is — and that he can get by with it. It gets to be sort of a disease."

Nella set the empty glass on the counter. "Could be I already have something to tell you that'll help."

Starbuck drew to attention. "Time's going to run out on me. If you have —"

"One of those men I was sitting with when you came in — drummers passing through. Said he didn't want to get mixed up in any of this, so he asked me to do his talking for him. He saw three horses in a shed at the end of the street."

A tautness gripped Starbuck. "He say exactly where?"

"In the alley back of that empty building on the corner."

Shawn sighed quietly, nodded. "Place is just below Lingo's office. Was by there a bit ago. He say when he saw them?"

"Late this afternoon. Was before dark. He was there looking at the building for some friend of his who's thinking about renting it for a store. It mean anything to you?"

"Plenty. Those horses could've been the ones that Yancey, Billy Joe Spicer, and Davis were riding. If they were it proves that Rufus was lying — that Yancey and his bunch were around a lot later than he claims. Backs up my belief that they were the ones who killed the sheriff. What I have to do is find Yancey. Any idea where he might be hiding out?"

Nella shook her head. "Hasn't been in here since the shooting — Greer's, I mean. Could be in town, but my guess is he's gone. His pa'd see to that."

"Expect you're right, but I'll have to make sure. Tell your drummer friend I'm obliged to him."

Shawn dropped a coin on the counter, turned for the door. He'd check the remaining saloons, the hotel, and a few other places that might come to mind, as well as the alley on that side of the street, but the possibility of turning up Yancey was slim, he felt. Likely that was the only thing that Rufus Lingo hadn't lied about — Yancey did leave Kennesaw; it was the hour that was at fault.

When morning came, all efforts within the settlement having proven futile, he'd widen the circle of the search, check with those families living in outlying precincts and see if any of them had noticed three riders passing by.

The only problem was that with daylight, and assuming his hunch and rumors were right, Dolan and the other councilmen would be in his office determined to take his star and authority. Starbuck shrugged off the probability. Let them. As far as he was concerned he'd still be a deputy.

11

Starbuck halted in the darkness at the corner of the Wagonwheel. Farther down the street the lamplight of other saloons shone yellow in the night, while from somewhere the tinkling notes of a piano floated gently through the warm hush.

After a time he moved on, conscious of the small hope of success earlier realized, but he was comforted somewhat by the knowledge that he had not failed completely. The information the drummer had given Nella bolstered his convictions, but it did nothing toward solving the problem about Yancey Lingo's present whereabouts — and that was the important issue.

Walking quietly down the deserted roadway that separated the facing rows of structures, Shawn let his eyes sweep from side to side. Shortly he slowed his step, abruptly alert. Deep within him a warning had sounded, and heeding such as always, he proceeded with deliberate care.

It could be Yancey — hiding along the street, on a rooftop, behind a second-floor window of a building, or in one of the dozen or more blackness-filled passageways that lay between many of the structures — waiting for the right moment to squeeze a trigger and put an end to the threat hanging over his head like a Damoclean sword.

Doing so would be easy — simple. In the night there would be no witness to ambush, and with a horse waiting close by, he could be away quickly, almost before the echoes of the gunshot had faded. And as far as blame was concerned, who would look to him? Rufus Lingo had convinced the townspeople that his son, grieving deeply, had ridden off and therefore could not possibly be suspected of involvement.

Starbuck halted, the hair on the back of his neck prickling. He was a fool, making himself so easy a target. He was simply inviting a bullet — if not from Yancey then from someone else either in Rufus Lingo's employ, or with a misplaced sense of devotion and loyalty and acting on his own — and getting cut down by a bullet would help nothing, especially Sam Culver and the law. It would be more sensible to pay the calls he had in mind by a more roundabout route.

Drawing in close to the wall of the building near which he stood, Shawn continued for a short distance and then turned into the dark void of the passageway that lay alongside it. Hesitating, he once more scanned the empty street, after which, moving carefully, he walked the length of the narrow weed-and-trash-littered corridor to the alley.

It was utterly dark along the rear of the structures and he could make out the area only indefinitely in the pale starlight. Crossing to the center of the wagon tracks, appearing bare and shining where the constant traffic of iron-tired wheels had set them apart from surrounding grassy growth, he resumed his slow march but with the feeling of impending danger still riding him.

He covered another twenty paces. A soft, solid thump somewhere behind him brought him to a stop. Hand dropping swiftly to the pistol on his hip, he spun. In the next instant he knew it was a mistake, that it had been a trick — a rock or some other object tossed to draw his attention.

Taut, Starbuck wheeled, met the onrush of three dark figures surging in on him from the rear of the store building to his left. He staggered as two of the men crashed into him, knocked him to his knees. He came upright fast, hearing rather than seeing the length of wood swishing through the air, aimed for his head. He threw up an arm, took the shocking blow on a shoulder.

Pain ripping through him, Shawn pivoted away, avoiding a second attempt by the shadowy shape crowding against him. Another of the attackers was suddenly behind him, hammering at his head, his neck, and his kidneys with rock-hard fists.

He spun again, striving to break out of such close quarters that hampered his own efforts. All of the training in expert boxing that Hiram Starbuck had given him was of no use here; this was strictly catch-as-catch-can, a full-fledged brawl where a man was faced with fighting and protecting himself as best as, and in any way, he could.

He lunged clear, turned, drove a fist into the belly of the man suddenly and unexpectedly before him, heard him grunt and saw him stumble away. A solid, hard-edged blow landed across his shoulders, almost dropped him again to his knees — the one with the length of wood. Cursing, he jerked aside, escaped the follow-up. A dim shape, hunched over and gasping for breath, was before him — the one he'd managed to sink his fist into.

Starbuck caught the man around the hips, whirled, sent him lurching into the others. There was a crash and a muffled oath as one of the pair staggered and fell onto a pile of trash.

Sucking for wind, beginning to feel the drain of strength, Shawn steadied himself and reached for his pistol. The holster was empty. The weapon had fallen out sometime during the attack. Grim, fists cocked, he rocked toward the nearest of the shifting shadows, sent a right driving into the man's body.

There was a howl of pain. A voice, low and labored, said: "Goddammit — use that there two by four!"

Shawn moved toward the speaker, aware now that the third man had recovered himself and had to be reckoned with. Ducking to one side, bobbing and weaving, he bore in on the men, now in a tight group. Dust was beginning to hang in the air, choking and filling his eyes, but if it was bothering him, he knew the others would have the same problem.

He made a quick, mock lunge at the man to his left, bore in instead on the one to the opposite side, had the satisfaction of feeling his knuckles smash solidly into skin and bone. A hand caught at his shoulder, yanked him half around. He took a flurry of stinging blows to the face, was at once conscious of the warm wetness of blood around his mouth.

Forsaking old Hiram's caution never to

permit anger to overtake him during a fight, Shawn rocked forward. He swung a left at the indistinct shape in front of him, followed with a right that missed. He weathered a blow to the belly, fell back a step, managed to halt one of his assailants crowding in on him with a stiffened arm.

In the next moment the one with the two by four timber struck him low on the neck, sent him to his knees. Immediately a booted foot came out of nowhere, caught him under the chin. He went over backward, sprawled flat in the dust. The length of wood whistled through the night once more. Shawn threw up an arm to protect his head. Blocked, the club glanced off, barely grazing its intended target.

A sharp toe dug into his ribs, his shoulder, still paining, was gradually stiffening from the punishment it had taken. He tried to roll away, received another brutal kick in the ribs. The club descended again, struck him solidly on the side of the head. His senses reeled.

Through dimming eyes Starbuck saw a square of light high up in the building nearby appear suddenly, vaguely heard an impatient voice call out.

"Hey — you damned drunks! Go do your fighting somewheres else!"

Shawn lay quiet, strength spent, a giddiness spinning his brain about in seemingly widening circles. He could hear nothing, was aware only of the gray darkness, the layers of floating dust.

He was alone. Finally he stirred, sat up. The three attackers had taken their satisfaction and hurried off. Body throbbing, head aching, Starbuck pulled himself upright. The effort brought a wave of nausea rushing through him, and for several moments he hung there, swaying precariously. It passed, and head now clearing, he glanced around until he located his pistol. Digging it out of the loose dust, he holstered it and started on down the alley. The jail was only a short distance away.

Reaching it, he entered, closed the door, and dropped the steel pin into the hasp. Drawing the shades, he stripped, and after first quelling the fire in his throat, took the bucket of water and washed himself off. He could do only half a job but it did make him feel better; tomorrow he'd go to the barber shop and indulge in a tub bath — assuming he was able to move.

Grinning wryly, Shawn picked up his blanket roll and carried it into the first cell. Tossing it onto the narrow cot provided, he locked the back door, still standing open, and then returned to the cage and sprawled on the hard bench. He was too tired to move into his quarters; he'd do that tomorrow, too, if he was still around.

12

Starbuck awoke early. For a time he lay motionless on the hard cot, considering his aches and pains, and then drew himself upright. That hot tub bath he had contemplated would go far toward erasing the stiffness and soreness that constrained his muscles, but second thought now warned him he'd best forego the treatment.

It would be smart to move out early — at once — and start his search for Yancey Lingo. By so doing he could avoid a showdown with Dolan and the town fathers, and if he was not available they certainly would find it impossible to reclaim his star and strip him of authority. He still felt they lacked the legal power to do so, but that might take days to determine, and if he could evade the issue he could pursue the hunt for Yancey without any complications.

Pulling on his clothing, he moved down the short hallway to the office and unlocked the door to the street. The flare of sunrise was filling the east with a pale gold sheen, and pausing in the opening, he glanced around. Two men were standing in front of

Dolan's Store, apparently waiting for the merchant. A third was groggily mounting his horse at the hitchrack of the Wagonwheel Saloon, homeward bound, no doubt, after a full night of revelry.

Anxious now to be on his way, Shawn dropped back into the room, crossed to the water bucket. It was empty, and snatching it up, he hurried down the corridor and out the back to the pump, where he filled the container. Slopping a quantity of the water over his face, which he found swollen and tender, he returned to the office, drying himself with his bandana en route.

Setting the bucket in its place, he picked up his hat, settled it gingerly on his head, and again paused, remembering the circumstances under which he had found his pistol. Jerking it from its holster, he examined it briefly, discovered its mechanism was gritty with sand, as he had feared. Muttering at the necessary delay, Starbuck crossed to the gunrack on the wall, snatched up one of the oily rags on its shelf, and fell to cleaning the weapon. The errand he was initiating was not one he cared to undertake with a faulty sixgun.

Finished, he slid the weapon into its holster, tossed the rag aside and swung toward the door. The thump of boot heels in the street brought him up short. It was too late. Silently cursing his luck, he stepped in behind the desk and sank into his chair, eyes on the doorway. Shortly, Dolan, accompanied by Ike Feathers and a man Shawn assumed to be Dave Bristow, entered.

Still-faced, they lined up in front of him. Only the livery stable owner's expression changed when they saw his battered features.

"What the red-hot hell happened to you?" he asked. Shawn smiled coldly. "Friends of the Lingos, I expect — or maybe of yours."

Dolan bristled. "Don't know anything about it, but I reckon it shows you how folks around here feel. Now maybe you'll listen to reason."

Starbuck shrugged. "If that means forgetting about Yancey, you're wasting breath."

"Suit yourself. Town council had a meeting last night. Voted to take your star, turn you out."

"You three the council?"

"Us and Rittenhouse and Bert Caldwell. Rittenhouse was the only one voting no. Majority rules. Now, we're willing to change our minds if you'll drop this foolishness about Yancey Lingo and start hunting the real killer."

"He's the killer, and you know it," Shawn said in disgust.

"Don't know nothing of the kind! You just think so, and that's likely because you and him got into it."

Starbuck stirred impatiently. He was in no mood to go over again the reasons why he knew Yancey was the guilty man.

"Want your answer now," the merchant said. "You can keep on wearing that star and being the deputy long as you get off Yancey's back. If you won't —"

"Obliged for the choice, but no thanks."

"Then I'll take your badge and you can figure yourself looking for a job."

Shawn reached for the bit of nickel, unpinned it, and tossed it to Dolan. "You've got it, but far as I'm concerned, I've still got a job and I aim to stay on it until I'm finished."

"You ain't working for us," Dolan replied, flushing angrily. "And we expect you to be moved out of here in one hour."

"Won't need that much time. Like for you to get this straight, however. Taking that star means nothing. I figure I'm still a deputy and will be until somebody higher up than you tells me different."

"Well, you ain't no deputy around this town!" Bristow said icily.

"Work for the whole county, not just you."

"This here's the headquarters and I reckon that gives us some rights," Dolan said. "You aiming to keep on dogging Yancey?"

Shawn nodded. "I swore to uphold the law."

Bristow brushed at the sweat on his swarthy face. "Hell, you can't do that! You got to look at this from our side. It'll hurt the town bad."

"Hurt it worse if you let a murderer get away with a killing."

"But you don't know that Yancey done it. Rufus said —"

"Don't bother to tell me what he said. Already know that he lied about one thing — about the time it was that Yancey and the others left town. Probably lied about a few more things, too."

He was on thin ice, Starbuck knew, more or less going on speculation and hunch, but he was positive that he was right. As he saw it, it was only a matter of getting Yancey and the two who sided him into a cell where they could not permanently disappear, and then finding the necessary proof for the law to convict them.

The councilmen regarded him silently for

a time and then Dolan shook his head. "Don't make no difference. We voted you out and we're standing by it. Want you out of here — and out of town."

"Out of this office, maybe," Starbuck said with a dry grin, "but not out of town — unless you figure you can handle the job of chasing me out."

Dolan's jaw hardened. "If I can't, I reckon I can get enough help to do it!" he snapped, and wheeling, started for the door. The other men, silent, turned and followed him into the street.

Unmoving, Shawn listened to the beat of their retreating footsteps in the early-morning quiet. Perhaps he was wrong; it could be that he no longer was a deputy, and he had no way of being sure. But there was doubt, and he intended to make use of that uncertainty and bring in Yancey Lingo and his friends before the matter could be decided one way or the other.

Sam Culver's murder was not something to be brushed under a rug and forgotten, just as the law was not a thing to be conveniently flaunted for the sake of one, or even several, individuals. Once that system was accepted, law and order would have no meaning and the country would soon revert to the way of the jungle.

He guessed he could accept Dolan's offer and drop the whole thing. It wasn't his town; he'd been in Kennesaw only a few days, probably would never stop there again, and it wasn't his fight. He'd been drawn into it by accident, and you couldn't say he had any close friends that were involved, unless you counted Sam Culver and Nella, both of whom were little more than acquaintances.

But still it was his fight, just as shooting a mad dog on the loose or blowing off the head of a six-foot diamondback about to strike some unwary passerby was his concern. A matter such as this — the murder of a man, any man, and the willful ignoring of the law — was the problem of everyone touched by it or not. He was obligated to make all such his business, otherwise all the years of living and dying of the persons who had labored to build a decent way of life for those who followed after went for nothing.

Putting open the top drawer of the desk, Shawn probed about until he found paper, pencil, and an envelope, and then set about writing a full report of Sam Culver's murder to Tom Spain, the U.S. marshal. He set forth his part in the affair, detailing the reasons why he believed Yancey Lingo was the killer, noting also the general attitude of the town as a whole and the councilmen in particular toward his bringing Yancey in for trial.

He mentioned also his position as deputy or ex-deputy, whichever it might be, and stated that he was acting on the basis that he still possessed the legal authority. He concluded the letter with the request the lawman come immediately to Kennesaw and be on hand so that there would be someone of undisputed standing to take charge when — and if — he returned with Lingo.

Folding the sheet, he sealed it in the envelope, addressed it to Spain in the Territorial capital. It would have to go by stagecoach mail, due to leave shortly, and thus should be posted immediately. Rising, he started for the door, paused. With Rufus Lingo's far-reaching power and influence, it might be safer not to entrust the report to the local office.

Deciding it was wise to be prudent in the matter, Shawn tucked the letter inside his shirt and walked quickly to Feather's livery barn. The stableman was not around, and bypassing the hostler, still dozing in the small cubicle that served as an office, he sought out the sorrel, saddled and bridled him, and rode out of the shadowy sprawling

111

structure by its rear door.

Cutting through the alley behind the buildings on the west side of the street, Starbuck reached the last and swung onto the road. He continued south for a quarter mile and there pulled to a halt in the shade of a tall, stringy mesquite. A half hour later he heard the rumble of the oncoming stagecoach and moved out to halt it.

The driver, swearing and frowning angrily, brought his half-broken horses to a halt. "What the devil, you —" he began, and then as Shawn passed the letter to him, along with one of his few remaining silver dollars, he settled back.

"Like for the marshal to get that soon as possible," Starbuck said. "Important business."

The old driver bucked his head. "For that there dollar I'll hand it to him myself."

"Be obliged if you will. When will you get to Prescott?"

"Around dark, the Lord willing. . . . Me and Tom Spain are friends. Know right where to find him. You the fellow I'm hearing all the bellyaching about?"

"Name's Starbuck. I'm Sam Culver's deputy."

"Was — according to what somebody said. But no mind, ain't nothing to me, and

I'll get your letter to Tom. Sure was too bad about Culver. Liked him. *Adios.*"

"So long," Shawn replied, pulling back and nodding to the faces peering at him from the interior of the coach as it lunged into motion.

He sighed. That much was done, and even if he failed for some reason, Tom Spain would have the details and facts of Culver's death and could take up where he left off.

Coming about, he struck for town at a steady lope. Now would begin the chore of tracking down Yancey Lingo, something he could expect no help with. It was something he would have to do on his own, and even then, if successful, he could only look forward to trouble. Rufus Lingo, with the support of the townspeople, would do everything possible to free his son. He could only hope that Spain would be on hand in Prescott when the letter arrived, and would read it and act immediately.

That, however, was something to think about later, if and when such developed. At the moment he was faced with the task of finding Yancey. He wasn't in town; subsequent events had convinced Shawn of that, and discounting Rufus Lingo's statement that his son, with Red Davis and Billy Joe

Spicer, had gone to some distant settlement to grieve over the death of Harley Greer, it was only logical to assume they would seek sanctuary in the place where the danger of betrayal would be the least likely — the Lingo ranch.

That's where he'd go next, Starbuck decided. He'd get a bite of breakfast and head out. The spread was some fifteen miles north of town, he recalled having been told.

13

Starbuck had no difficulty locating the Lingo ranch. It lay in a broad, green valley, protected on the north and west by low, palisaded mountains, bordered in the east by a fast-running stream and the south by a broad plain covered with brush and scrub cedars. A wide rock-pillared gate supporting a foot-thick timber, from which, by chains, hung a carved board bearing the name of the owner, designated the entrance.

Halted in the fairly dense growth in the crest of a rise, Shawn studied the scatter of buildings making up the ranch. One fairly large structure, recently painted with a coat of white, was undoubtedly the main house. A long, flat-roofed affair beyond and across the hardpack would be the crew's quarters. The cook shack was easily identifiable by its smokestack. A large barn with connected wagon shed and a dozen other lesser buildings made up the remainder. The place had a swept, efficient look to it, would have appeared utterly bleak were it not for the large, spreading cottonwood trees that ringed the grounds.

Getting into it unseen would be practically impossible, despite the fact that it was midmorning and most of the hands would be on the range at work, or, if members of the night crew, in the bunkhouse catching their sleep. He could figure on the cook, the yard help, and a housekeeper along with Yancey Lingo, Davis, and Spicer, assuming his hunch concerning them was correct. That Rufus Lingo himself could be around was also a possibility, but Shawn doubted that; more than likely the older member of the family spent the major portion of time in Kennesaw, visited the ranch only on occasions.

Under cover of darkness making his way to the house would be no chore. Considerable brush lay to the south of the buildings, and a man could approach from that direction, being faced as he drew near the structures with but a narrow stretch of cleared ground. Waiting until nightfall was out of the question, however; if it developed that Yancey wasn't there he would have wasted an entire day — and time now had become a precious commodity not to be squandered.

He would have to take a chance, depend on the absence or the preoccupation of the hired help to permit his slipping into the ranch and making an arrest of Yancey and his two partners. The latter could be accomplished if he encountered no more opposition than the cook and one or two others; bucking half a dozen or so armed punchers in the effort would be something else.

Touching the sorrel with his spurs, Starbuck dropped back into the cedars and swung wide to the south. Then, cutting due north, he moved toward the blind side of the house. That he could be seen from the barn and that portion of the yard lying in front of it was something that could not be avoided.

He reached the corner of the larger building with no trouble, halted in the shadow of the structure. A hammering was coming from inside the barn and he could hear the occasional rattle of pans in the cook shack, which stood directly ahead on his left. The ranchhouse itself, blinds drawn, lay in silence. Either there was no one inside or those that were still slept.

Abruptly a door squeaked open, banged shut. Starbuck stiffened in the saddle. A moment later an elderly man, dirty, white apron covering his front, appeared, a dishpan of water in his hands. He slopped its gray contents against the trunk of a nearby tree, turned, paused as he saw Shawn. Surprise lifted his straggling brows.

"Now, who'n tarnation are you?"

Starbuck breathed easier, grinned. The cook didn't know him, which was to be expected, since he'd been around for only a few days. But the old man could have been in town, chanced to see him.

"Name's Ben," he said, choosing the one foremost in his mind. He'd have to bluff, play his cards as they fell. "This the Lingo place?"

"Reckon so — all hundred thousand acres of it. Didn't you see the signs?"

"What signs?"

"The big one hanging over the gate, and a bunch more saying 'No Trespassing.' "

"Missed them all, seems. Come across the flat."

"Well, you're here. What'd'you want?"

"Looking for work — punching cows, breaking broncs, whatever's open."

The old man wagged his head. "Foreman ain't here, and you'd best see Mr. Lingo, anyhow. He generally does the hiring and firing."

Shawn nodded thoughtfully. "I see. . . . Sure could use a cup of coffee."

The cook shrugged, wiped at the sweat on his beet-red features with a corner of the apron. "Expect I can spare a cup or two. Step down and come in."

Starbuck dismounted, tied the gelding to

a clump of rabbitbush, and followed the man into the kitchen, prickling hot from the big Old Homestead range going full-blast in one corner. The cook motioned to one of the chairs at the end of a small table, preferring to serve his unexpected guest there rather than in the adjoining room, where a much larger affair was set up for the crew's use.

Setting a cup before Shawn, he filled it from a granite pot that bore the baked-on stains of long usage, said, "Sugar 'n milk?"

"Black's fine. . . . Sure smells good," Starbuck said, and took a sip of the steaming liquid. Nodding, he added, "Tastes mighty good, too."

The older man smiled. "Ain't never had no complaints. Where you from, Ben?"

"Here and there — mostly north. This Mr. Lingo — his front name Yancey?"

The cook shook his head. "Naw, Yancey's the boy. Rufus is the one you got to talk to — he's his pa. You know Yancey?"

"Met once in a saloon."

"Offered you a job, I bet."

"Sort of. He around anywhere?"

"Nope. Was by last night, him and a chum of his."

Starbuck gave that due consideration. "By here — that mean he was going somewhere?"

"Yeh. Had me rustle them up some grub and grabbed their bedrolls. Headed for that hideout shack they got up on the mesa, I figured. Prob'ly picking themselves up a coupla gals from one of the saloons and aiming to have themselves a big time. Yancey's a great one for that."

Shawn nodded. That much was now definite — Lingo was not there. But the trip had not gone for nothing; he had something to go on. The impulse to ask the elderly man about the hideout shack, its location, came to his lips, but he let it pass. Best not to press the cook too hard; it could arouse suspicion — and someone in town would know of its location. Besides, he should move on, get clear of the Lingo ranch before his luck ran out and he encountered someone who recognized him.

Draining his cup, Starbuck rose, grinned. "Sure obliged to you for the good coffee. Don't often run across a man who knows how to make it right. . . . Mr. Lingo, I'll find him in town?"

"Expect so. Now, you could wait for Jack Snider, he's the foreman, was you not in a hurry."

"No hurry, but I'd sort of like to look over the town, anyway. Yancey shows up again you might tell him I dropped by."

"He ain't apt to — not for three, maybe four days."

"Well, maybe I'll bang into him somewhere," Shawn said and turned to the door. "Obliged to you again."

"You're welcome, Ben," the old cook replied, and then continued, "I know it ain't none of my business, but did you walk yourself into a thrashing machine or something?"

"Or something," Starbuck said. "Me and three other jaspers had us a sort of a disagreement."

"Was I guessing, I'd say they won," the cook said. "Good luck."

"Same to you," Shawn answered, and stepping out into the yard, circled back to the sorrel.

Mounting, he cut quickly across the open ground and ducked into the brush, placing it between himself and the ranch, unwilling to press his good fortune any farther than necessary. Gaining a safe distance, he slowed, looked over his shoulder. There was no one in sight, no one following.

He drew a long breath. The visit to the Lingo ranch had paid off. All that was necessary now was to find out where the mesa with its hideout shack was located. Yancey, along with Billy Joe Spicer and Red Davis, would be there — and arresting the three of them should not be difficult.

But he must use care and not tip his hand — ask questions only of someone who he knew would not relay his interest to Rufus Lingo. He could think of only one person he could trust — Nella.

14

Kennesaw appeared deserted when Shawn turned into its main street. The noon hour, he guessed, with everyone home having dinner, but when he reached the town's center he saw the collection of persons at the cemetery just beyond Ahab York's church and realized the funeral of Sam Culver was being held.

He swung the sorrel about at once and rode to the fenced-in plot of ground with its wooden crosses and stone markers, dismounted, and quietly made his way to the gathering.

There were two graves — Culver's and Harley Greer's. It was ironic — outlaw and lawman being buried side by side — but he guessed it didn't matter, since, in death, the difference in men disappeared. Removing his hat, Starbuck took up a position at the rear of the medium-sized crowd, listening as the Reverend York intoned all the appropriate phrases.

Idly running his eyes over the assembly, Shawn located several of the men he now knew: Whitcomb of the Wagonwheel

Saloon, banker Matt Rittenhouse, Feathers, Dolan, Doc Grey, Bristow — Rufus Lingo.

He studied the land broker thoughtfully. There was a look of solemn, respectful grief on the man's features, further accented by the black suit he had donned for the occasion. Like as not he had served as one of the pallbearers, Shawn assumed with a touch of bitterness; the father of the murderer acting as escort to the murdered.

Shifting his eyes, Starbuck brought them to a halt as they fell upon Sarah. She was standing with a group of elderly women behind her father. Dressed entirely in white, head covered like the others with a prim sun-shielding bonnet, she appeared much older than before.

Her gaze lifted to meet his, held, sober and noncommittal, and then she looked away as the deep-timbred voice of her father ceased. With the other women she took a step forward, toward the two graves, and lifting their faces to the clean blue overhead, they began to sing: *"On a hill faraway, stands an old rugged cross . . ."*

In the hot, bright sunshine the words floated sweetly across the hushed yard, mingled with the cheery whistling of a meadowlark in a nearby field. Starbuck's thoughts slipped back over the years to another church, its adjoining cemetery, and a small choir rendering a similar hymn while they lowered his mother into the ground. Those had been different times for him, for Ben, and for Hiram, their father, who, hardbitten, close to the realities of nature and the uncertainties of life as he was, had taken the loss of his wife hard.

The last of the haunting notes faded. Sarah and the women stepped back. Ahab York droned a benediction, and then slowly, reluctantly, the crowd began to break up, turn toward the street. Shawn, replacing his hat, cut back to where the sorrel waited, pleased that he had been able to attend the services for Culver. Now if he could bring the lawman's killer to justice he would feel that he had discharged his obligations fully.

Swinging onto the gelding, Shawn started to pull off, conscious of the townspeople moving past him, of their close, hostile looks as he glanced their way. Shrugging indifferently, he continued, caught a glimpse of Sarah walking slowly in the direction of the parsonage that stood near the church. He would have liked to talk with her again, but this was not the place, or the time.

Back on the street, he crossed over and

drew in at the hitchrack fronting the Wagonwheel. The doors were closed in deference to the funerals, but when he tried the handles he found them unlocked and entered. Nella, with a bartender and two other women, was at a table. All turned as he approached. Nella smiled and the aproned man rose to his feet, headed toward the bar.

"Reckon the planting's done so we're open for business again," he said. "That right?"

Shawn nodded, and motioning to the blond girl, sat down at a different table, waving off the questioning look of the bartender, now at his usual station.

"Were you there?" Nella asked, sinking into a chair opposite Starbuck.

He nodded again. "Quite a crowd."

"I never go to funerals. Expect the only one I ever will go to will be my own — and that'll be because I won't have any say about it."

Starbuck grinned wryly. "From the attention I got I think they'd as soon have been burying me."

Nella brushed at her hair. "That's the way they feel about you. Plenty of them are sure it was you that shot Sam Culver and are trying to throw the blame on Yancey."

126

"Been told that to my face. Some of the crowd that showed up at the jail saw me looking at the sheriff's fingers. Wanted to see if he had made those marks on the floor purposely."

"But they think you were using his fingers to do it —"

"That's what they decided. No sense to it. Culver was my friend. I had no reason to kill him."

"Way they see it you saw the chance to get his job. Being the deputy, you'd be in line to take over."

"That kind of logic comes from Rufus Lingo or the reverend —"

"Hadn't you heard it before?"

"It was mentioned last night, too, but it's not worth losing any sleep over. If they were sure of it, I expect they'd be doing something about it."

Nella raised her gaze, looked beyond him. Pete Whitcomb had returned, was fastening back the inside doors. Other men were entering.

"They intend to — I wanted to see you, tell you that." She paused, considered him critically. "Did you have some trouble? Your face is swelled, and there's bruises —"

"A little," he replied, running fingers lightly over his stubble of beard. "Got jumped after I left here last night. Three men."

"Who?"

He shrugged, explored the lump on his head gingerly. "Can't say. It was too dark."

"Expect I can find out if you like —"

"Never mind, no damage done. There is one thing I'd like to ask you. Did you ever hear of a hideout that Yancey Lingo has on some mesa?"

Nella's lips tightened. "I've been there," she murmured.

The recollection was evidently distasteful to her. Shawn let it ride for a bit and then said: "Can you tell me how to find it?"

"Sure. It's a place near the end of the mountains west of town. Sort of stands out from the rest of the hills, like a big, round knob."

"How far?"

"Twenty-five, maybe thirty miles. Why?"

"Got a hunch that's where Yancey and the others are holed up. Aim to go see."

Alarm filled her eyes. "You can't — you won't be able to! The sides of the mesa are straight up and down and there's only one trail leading to the top. The shack sets right there at the end of it."

"No brush or anything to hide behind?"

"Not much. Shawn, you'd never reach

the shack without them seeing you — shooting you. I know because I was there for several days."

It would have been one of Yancey Lingo's parties, Starbuck supposed, but he did not pursue the subject. "Could be I can find another way up. Any idea how high the mesa is?"

Nella sighed, shook her head. "I'm no judge of something like that. Three or four times as high as this saloon, I'd say. Are you going to try and climb it? I don't think —"

"I'll have to have a look at it, anyway."

She was silent for a time, the concern on her features deepening. "When are you going?" she asked finally.

"Right away," he said, and pushed back from the table.

Impulsively she reached out, laid her hand on his arm. "Shawn, it's foolish — risky. I'm afraid you —"

"Don't worry about it. I'm not loco enough to let them potshot me, but if Yancey's up there, I have to get him, along with Spicer and Davis — somehow. Seems I have to if the town's getting big ideas about hanging Sam Culver's murder on me."

"You could just wait. Yancey's bound to show up in a few days."

"That might not be soon enough,"

Starbuck said and rose to his feet. "I'll be obliged if you'll keep what we've been talking about to yourself."

"Of course," the girl said, coming upright also. She glanced around. The patronage of the saloon was increasing. "When will I see you?"

"Tomorrow, likely," he answered, and ignoring the hard looks of several men just entering, moved through the doorway out onto the porch.

Mounting the sorrel, he rode down the street to the jail, swung off, and hurried inside. His gear was where he had tossed it, and picking it up, he returned to the gelding, secured it to his saddle. Going again into the office, he searched about until he found a coil of rope, a lariat that had somehow come into the lawman's possession. He nodded in satisfaction. It, added to his own, should provide length enough for whatever use he might have.

Once more alongside the sorrel, Shawn hung the coil with that already tied to his saddle, and mounted. Swinging about, he halted abruptly, a tremor of surprise coursing through him. Directly across, standing in the shadow of the vacant building where she could not be seen by anyone on the street, was Sarah York.

Kneeing the gelding, he moved to her. She was still clad in the crisp white dress and the pert bonnet he had seen earlier, but now her features were troubled.

"Shawn —"

He came off the saddle, aware that she was studying him closely, taking note of the swelling and bruises on his face. Question was in her eyes.

"It's nothing," he said before she could ask. "Is there something wrong?"

"I'm afraid so," she answered in a faltering voice. "I had to warn you. The town council — and Papa — have sent for a marshal. They're going to arrest you for the murder of the sheriff."

It had cost her much to tell him that, Starbuck knew, since in a sense it would be betraying her father.

"Thanks. . . . The marshal, is it the one in Prescott?"

"No, in Cartertown." She hesitated, glanced over the gear on the sorrel. "Are you leaving?"

"For a while. Expect to be back." He was not sure it was wise to take her fully into his confidence — not that he felt she would intentionally reveal his plans, but he feared Ahab York's influence over her.

"Maybe it would be best if you didn't. If

131

you aren't here they couldn't arrest you."

"Wouldn't take them long to pass the word, turn me into a wanted man, and I don't want that. I didn't shoot Sam Culver. Hope you believe that."

"I do, but Mr. Lingo is talking it up strong and people are listening to him."

"Guess that's only natural, since it was his son that did it."

"Is that where you're going now — to find him?"

Shawn nodded. "Hoping to."

Sarah bit at her lips, looked down. "Please — be careful," she said in a faint voice, and wheeling hurriedly, walked back along the shaded wall of the empty structure.

Starbuck watched her for a time and then remounted the sorrel. Sarah was a strange girl, one seemingly torn between loyalty to herself and to her father. He wished there was some way he could help.

Returning to the street, he looked beyond the buildings to the mountains in the west. At their lower end, Nella had said, and from the description she had given, the mesa where he hoped to find Yancey Lingo and his friends should not be difficult to locate.

15

It was near midafternoon when Starbuck found the mesa. The formation, rising like a thick thumb from the surrounding land, was much nearer the range of hills than he had anticipated, and that had caused him to swing farther south than necessary.

Keeping the sorrel in behind the intervening clumps of brush as much as possible, he rode in close. From the lower level he could see no sign of the shack built on the crest, and he logically supposed any occupants, if indeed there were some, would be unable to get a glimpse of him. He took no chance, however, and made use of all available cover until he pulled to a halt at the rock-strewn base of the monolithic upthrust.

The sides were steep, as Nella had said they would be, but climbing to the summit with the aid of ropes appeared possible. He would first have a look at the trail, though; it might be that with care he could manage to reach the shack by that route.

Walking the sorrel slowly to hold down the sound of their passage in the loose shale and crackling dry brush, Shawn circled around to where he could see the narrow slope rising steeply on the west. Dismounting, he tied the gelding to a clump of greasewood and proceeded the remainder of the way on foot, taking care to keep in close.

Gaining the foot of the trail, he crawled behind a large boulder that, storm-released at some time in the past, had tumbled down the grade and come to rest at the bottom. Removing his hat, he raised his head cautiously.

He could see the upper portion of the shack's front wall and the overhang of the roof. The sagging structure was placed, as he'd been told, near the lip of the mesa and was in such a position as to afford anyone in it a constant view of the pathway leading up from the flat. The slope, except for a few small rocks scattered here and there, was sparsely covered with short brown grass and devoid of rabbitbush, sage, and other similar clump growth.

He would have to resort to scaling the palisade-like walls. Shawn shook his head, considering the necessity. It would be a difficult chore, a dangerous one, and he wasn't even sure Yancey and the others were there; he was going strictly on what the Lingo ranch cook had assumed.

Brushing at the sweat lying on his face, Starbuck studied the slanting trail. There was a low ridge of rock and weeds some twenty feet or so farther up. He probably could make it to that point unnoticed, but there it would end. Nothing large enough to conceal even a small animal, much less a man, lay beyond that. But if he could reach it, odds were good that he'd have a better view of the cabin and perhaps be able to see if it was occupied.

He decided it was worth the risk. Removing his spurs, and hunched low, Shawn gathered his breath, moved hurriedly up the slope, and pulled in behind the berm. Waiting out several moments, he peered over its edge. Disappointment rolled through him. He was only a little better off than below, as the lower two-thirds of the shack was still not visible to him. Swiping again at the sweat misting his eyes, he lay back, swore softly. He'd —

Abruptly a tight grin pulled at his mouth. A shout followed by a burst of laughter floated down the grade. Someone was in the shack — and it could only be Yancey, along with Billy Joe Spicer, Red Davis, and probably several women recruited to spend the time with them if the old cook was to be again believed.

Satisfied, he wormed his way back to the boulder and on to the base of the slope. Still careful to keep well down, he retraced his steps to the sorrel, and not bothering to strap on his spurs but hanging them on the saddlehorn, mounted. Wheeling, he cut back along the foot of the towering formation, eyes scanning its vertical walls for a possible course to the crest, one preferably a fair distance from the point where the shack was perched.

He found what he sought a short time later — a narrow gash where rainwater poured off the summit during the occasional storms that lashed the area. Leaving the sorrel securely tied in a clump of cedars, Shawn took both coils of rope from the saddle, and hanging one around his neck, the other over a shoulder, started up the cleft.

He climbed the first few yards with no difficulty and then came to a halt, finding himself faced with a sheer rise of considerable distance. Shaking out the shorter lariat, he studied the jagged wall. A finger of rock jutting forth from one side of the gash offered possibilities.

Balancing himself, he made a pass at the finger with his loop, missed. Patient, he tried again, and once more the rope fell short. On the third attempt the circle settled around the small pinnacle. Drawing the line taut, he tested it with his weight. It appeared solidly anchored.

Taking a few moments to catch his breath and sleeve away the sweat, Starbuck grasped the rope firmly and started upward, climbing it hand over hand while he braced himself against the sides of the cliff with his feet.

He reached the finger heaving for wind, body soaked from the effort. Leaning against the cool rock, he waited until his breathing was again normal and then, freeing the lariat, glanced upward. He could ascend for perhaps another ten feet and then it would be necessary to use the rope again.

Doggedly he attacked the rain-smoothed slash once more, pulling and clawing his way until he was compelled to halt because of the wall's sheerness. Shaping another loop, he considered the cut from this different position. There was no convenient crag to make use of this time, only smooth, low knobs around which a loop would drop only to slide off quickly.

His eyes paused on a large boulder a bit to the side of the gash. If he could drop his rope over it he would have solid purchase, but the fact that the rock was some distance to the left of the cut could mean trouble. Once he put his weight on the line, he would throw himself off balance and swing, pendulum-like, against a ledge. If he collided with sufficient force, he could lose his grip and drop to the rocks below.

He had no choice but to risk it. Bracing himself squarely in order to make the throw, Starbuck sent his loop snaking up and to the side. The noose dropped over the boulder on the first try. He grinned wryly as he pulled it taut; that had been easy — too easy, in fact — could be a portent of bad luck. Making certain his pistol was securely in its holster, he drew his hat farther down on his head, and taking a hitch around his left wrist with the rope, he locked both hands about the tough strands and began to climb.

Immediately he rocked to one side as gravity and the angle of the lariat's suspension combined to pull him off his feet. He went to both knees, off balance, spun crazily out into space, and arced across the face of the wall, the rope scraping noisily along the rough edge of the shelf below the boulder.

Starbuck felt himself being hurled toward the side of the formation. Frantically shifting his weight, he caused his body to twist and instantly thrust forth both legs. He grunted as his feet came solidly against the granite slab. For a brief time he hung there as relief ran through him; if he hadn't managed to turn, had taken the impact instead on a shoulder or his head, the search for Yancey Lingo would have ended with him lying dead or badly injured on the rocks.

The muscles of his arms began to throb. He glanced upward. It was about ten feet to the shelf, probably another twenty up its slanting surface to the rock where he'd anchored the rope.

Calling on reserve strength, Shawn began the climb, legs dangling, to the lip of the ledge and hauled himself onto it. Again he paused, clinging to the rope, gasping for breath while he recovered. Five minutes later he resumed the ascent, crawling as he pulled himself along the taut line. It was much easier on the sloping slab of granite, since the entire weight of his body was not being put on his arms alone.

But the risk taken had paid off. Freeing the lariat from the rock, he looked ahead. A long sheet of smooth rock was before him, at the upper end of which was another sturdy boulder. Beyond it he could see the gray-green of grass and weeds.

Swinging the loop, Shawn connected with the rock, walked himself up by drawing in the rope hand over hand until he had reached it. A sigh escaped him as he coiled the lariat. The flat crest of the mesa was only a few steps away.

16

Slinging the rope over his shoulder as before, Starbuck moved onto the plateau. The shack was not visible because of the cedars and clumps of brush, and he pushed on, walking fast but carefully over the fairly level ground.

A short time later he halted, dropped into a crouch. The weather-grayed structure was suddenly before him, perched on the forward edge of a small clearing. Hunkered behind a mound of weedy rocks, he studied it.

An uncovered window faced him; he could see none in the adjacent wall, guessed there would be none on the opposite member either as miners constructed their domiciles with the thought in mind of obtaining maximum warmth in the winter months while giving no consideration to ventilation. The door would be in the side farthest from him.

He could hear the low murmur of voices, punctuated now and then with a quickly blurted oath or laughter, and the sharp click of cards indicated a game in progress. Assuring himself there was no one outside the structure, Shawn moved out from behind the mound and crossed to the window. Removing his hat, he drew in close to the opening and looked into the room.

Yancey, Red Davis, and Billy Joe Spice. . . . He grinned in satisfaction. There were no women present. The men were seated on makeshift chairs around a rickety table playing poker. Each had a bottle of whiskey at his elbow and a pile of matches before him serving as money.

In one corner a small, flat-topped cookstove stood cold with a frying pan and a coffee pot on its four-holed surface. Nearby, on a bench nailed into the wall, were unwashed dishes, cups, and a supply of grub. Bedrolls, still in disarray, as if they had just been quitted, lay upon three of the double bunks.

"Try dealing some decent cards for a change, dammit." It was Red Davis. His voice was low, peevish. Billy Joe laughed. "That ain't the way for a man to win. Got to deal hisself the good cards."

Starbuck squatted below the portlike window. Since the three had no female company the problem of getting them down from the mesa and back to Kennesaw was diminished somewhat, but it would still be difficult and dangerous. He could expect plenty of trouble, especially from Red Davis.

And binding their wrists behind their backs and leading them in like a string of pack mules was not the exact solution, thanks to Rufus Lingo and the townspeople who were lined up with him. To avoid gunplay, which would only defeat the purpose of arrest where the three men were concerned should he be compelled to shoot one, it would be best to enter the town quietly and unseen, and lie low until U.S. Marshal Spain put in an appearance — all of which would be no small accomplishment. He could expect to have his hands full.

Too full, Starbuck decided. Better to play it safe. After all, it was Yancey Lingo he was most concerned with; the others, too, of course since they undoubtedly were witnesses to the murder of Sam Culver and likely would talk freely when made to see the shadow of the scaffold looming over them. He would need them, that was certain, but Yancey was the important one — and one rabbit in the stewpot was worth three still in the brush.

Mind made up, Starbuck rose, looked around for the horses. He located them under a lean-to a short way to the west of the shack. He had no way of knowing which mount was Lingo's, but selected the one with the most expensive gear. The saddles had not been removed from the animals, a loosening of the cinch having been deemed sufficient, along with slipped bridles.

Tightening the band and restoring the bit and headstall to the horse, a husky, white-stockinged bay, Shawn then took one of his ropes and cut it into several lengths. That done, he gathered up the pieces, and taking the reins of the bay, returned quietly to the cabin.

He could hear Yancey and the redhead arguing as he circled the small structure and halted on its nearest blind side. Tieing the bay to a stump where he would be handy, he dropped back to the window.

"Weren't my fault!" Davis was protesting in a dogged voice. "They just wouldn't come."

Lingo swore in disgust. "Well, we sure'n hell can't just set around here playing stud and yakking for three or four days. I'll go plumb loco! . . . How much money'd you offer them?"

"Ten dollars apiece —"

"Then why the hell —"

Davis shrugged. "One of them, one that calls herself Trixie, she said there wasn't enough money in the country to get her up here again, said once was plenty."

"Maybe you ought to trot over there and talk to them yourself, Yancey," Billy Joe suggested, idly shuffling the deck of dog-eared cards. "You always was a good talker and they might listen to you."

Lingo scrubbed at his whisker-covered chin. "Just might do that, come dark."

"Be smarter to go clean over to Yanktown," Davis said. "They don't know you — us there."

"Too dang far," Yancey said, wagging his head. "Hell, them gals've got a price. They'll come was I to offer enough cash."

Davis shrugged his thick shoulders. "Sure, they want the cash, they just don't want the horsing around they figure they'll get. . . . When you figure your pa'll be showing up?"

Yancey leaned back in his chair, yawned, stretched. "You heard him, same as me. Few days."

"What's he waiting on?"

"Expect he's got a idea about that deputy — aiming to have him turn up dead somewheres."

"No need stashing us away for that. We could've handled him ourselves — like we done the sheriff."

"Like I done," Lingo corrected pointedly.

"But I reckon Pa knows what he's doing. Always does."

Billy Joe laughed. "He sure didn't cotton much to what you done to the sheriff! Thought he was going to bust a blood vessel there for a minute when you told him!"

"Sort've surprised him. He didn't figure I could do something like that. . . . Hell, was easy."

Starbuck listened, mentally taking down all that was being said that related to the killing of Culver. It had been Yancey himself who had triggered the bullet, just as the lawman had indicated, or tried to indicate, before he died.

"Too bad that there smart-alec deputy wasn't around at the time," Spicer said. "You could've finished him off, too."

"Still hoping for the chance," Yancey replied, his face darkening. "If Pa don't fix him somehow and he's still around when we get back, I aim to look him up."

"Won't be no cinch," Davis warned. "You see how quick he drawed and blasted Harley? Faster'n anybody I've ever seen."

"Maybe, but there's ways of getting around that," Lingo said smugly, reaching for his bottle of liquor. He took a short swallow, smacked appreciatively. "Always say a man can skin any snake that comes along if he sets his mind to it. Just got to do some outsmarting."

Shawn reached down for the pistol on his hip, drew, and checked the loads. He'd heard enough — all that he needed to know that he was right. What remained now was to get Yancey and his two friends safely back to Kennesaw where they could be locked up and held for trial.

"Can't see no sense waiting for dark before I go after them women. Might just as well go now."

At Yancey's voice and the sudden thump of his chair as he let it tip forward to all four legs, Starbuck turned. Pistol in one hand, lengths of rope in the other, he passed silently along the wall of the shack to its forward corner. From inside came Billy Joe's whiny tones.

"Let's all go. Ain't no need for me and Red to hang around here."

Shawn crossed the front of the cabin in two long strides, swung into the doorway, halted.

"I'm changing your plans," he said coolly, drifting the muzzle of his forty-five back and forth over them. "Raise your hands — high!"

17

Ahab York, standing at the window inside Dolan's store, watched Starbuck walk out of the Wagonwheel Saloon, mount his big sorrel horse, and ride down the center of the street to the jail, where he dismounted and entered.

Indignation and anger stirred him. Starbuck, representing all that was wrong, all that was evil in Kennesaw, had no right to do that. The town council had dismissed him, had taken away his badge and authority, and it was only a matter of time until the lawman they had sent for would arrive and arrest him for the murder of Sheriff Culver. The gall of the man — parading around, insolent as you please! It was a mockery to decent folks! Why, he'd even showed up at the funeral service! But that was the makeup of his kind — bold as brass.

He hoped the Cartertown marshal would get there soon. This Starbuck was having a bad effect on Sarah. He saw it in her eyes, in the absent way she went about doing things, in the rising of her color whenever she happened to be near him. His Sarah! It was hard to understand — his own daughter, always so obedient, so shy, suddenly finding attraction in a man who stood for all that was bad, that he was against.

He supposed he had to admit that Starbuck was the sort of man a woman would find interesting, and possibly could fall in love with. Tall, dark, with gray-blue eyes and a way about him that gave the impression of strength and an easygoing recklessness, no doubt he could be termed a handsome man. He spoke, too, as one who'd been educated a bit better than average, and when you put it all together it wasn't hard to see how he could turn the head of a sheltered girl like Sarah.

He had talked to her about him, pointing out the one unforgivable fault that outshone any of the virtues she might see in him — that he was a killer, a murderer, and that, in the sight of God, was the worst sin of all. He had forbade her ever to talk to the man again, even to think of him, for once stirred by base thoughts the mind all too often persuaded the conscience to follow a wrong path.

Sarah had listened in that quiet, patient way of hers and then gone on about her housework, saying neither yea nor nay, and for the first time in their relationship he had found himself at a loss to cope with her. Later, thinking on it, he reckoned it was because, also for the first time, the girl believed she was in love. York sighed deeply, wished his wife were still alive to share the problem.

But his worries would soon be over — if he could just manage to keep Sarah in hand until then. Rufus had assured him that Starbuck would get his just rewards, once the arrest was made — and a man could rely on his promises. He was a good man, this Rufus Lingo, and a generous one. It was too bad Yancey was so unlike his father. He and Sarah would make a fine pair.

He wasn't going to give up on that idea yet. Wasn't there a passage in the Bible about young men sowing their wildness and then settling down to a life of hard work? Or had he read that in the *Minister's Monitor*? He'd have to look it up the first chance he got, maybe even preach a sermon on it. Who knows, it just might turn Yancey around, start things going the other way. He'd have to get Yancey into the church first, however, so that he could hear it. Perhaps he could work that part out with Rufus, tell him the service was just for Yancey and enlist his aid in having the boy on hand. No doubt Rufus would be pleased with the idea.

Ahab York's wandering thoughts came to a halt. Starbuck had reappeared. He was carrying his saddlebags and blanket roll, and began to lash them down on his saddle. That done, he reentered the jail, returned shortly with a large coil of rope, which he added to his own. Evidently the man was leaving Kennesaw. Frowning, York called to Dolan, working behind the back counter of the store.

"That murderer's riding out! Lawman you sent for's not going to get here in time."

The merchant dropped whatever he was engaged in, came forward at once to the minister's side. "Sure looks that way," he admitted. Then, "Well, there ain't nothing we can do about it."

"We could stop him —"

Dolan looked curiously at York. "You want to be the one that tries it? I don't think you'll find anybody else around here anxious to get his head blowed off."

York was silent, admitting to the truth. Dolan swung away. "Let him go. They'll put out wanted dodgers and catch him soon enough."

Starbuck was climbing onto his saddle. He settled himself, wheeled about, halted, his attention caught by something or someone across the street that was hidden from view by the buildings. After a moment or two Starbuck rode to that point and was also lost to sight.

That was a strange thing for a man leaving town to do. There were no roads lying in that direction; Starbuck should have ridden either down the street if he was planning to go west or south, or back up past the stores if he had it in mind to go north or east.

Ahab started to call this to Ed Dolan's attention when Starbuck moved into the open once again. He rode from the side of the building into the clear, cut left, and continued on his way.

Vague fear rose within York. Starbuck had paused to talk with someone — someone he had evidently not expected, and from the way that person had so carefully remained out of sight, it was apparent that he — or she — did not wish to be seen by others. Who could it have been? Starbuck had no friends in town that he knew of except that saloon girl, Nella or whatever her name was — and she certainly would not have taken such precautions. Brazen as she was, she would have walked right up and entered the jail while he was there. Who, then? *Could it have been Sarah?*

The thought came to York with the suddenness of a thunderbolt. He felt himself

152

pale, and abruptly tense, pivoted to the door. Brushing through it without comment to Dolan, he hurried off the porch, and crossing the street in long, storklike steps, strode purposefully down a passageway that would lead him to the alley lying behind the structures on the opposite side. If it had been Sarah that Starbuck was talking to he would be able to intercept her as she made her way home.

He reached the alley, halted. A mixture of anger and frustration surged through him. Sarah, face tipped down, was moving toward him. Composing himself, York waited until she was almost abreast and then stepped into the open.

"You have been talking to that murderer!" he said in a barely controlled voice. "I saw you — him."

The girl pulled up short at his unexpected appearance. Her eyes flared with surprise and a measure of fear, and then she shrugged.

"I won't deny it, Papa."

"I asked — told you never to go near him again, but you have disobeyed me. Why?"

She did not look up. "I — I love him."

"Love!" Ahab York shouted the word. "What do you know of love — and for a man like him — an evil man!"

"I don't believe that. He's not evil."

"You dare question me? You think you know more of men than I?"

"I know Shawn better than you," Sarah replied evenly.

"How can you? You've only seen him once or twice, hardly talked to him —"

"I just feel it," she said simply. "I believe you're letting your friendship for Mr. Lingo color your thoughts about Shawn." Sarah paused, as if to muster courage. "Are you sure you don't feel toward him the way you do because you're afraid you'll lose Mr. Lingo's support of the church and all the things he's promised to give?"

"Sarah!"

"I can't help it, Papa. I think that's why you're so against Shawn and why you won't give him a chance to talk to you, explain why he's the way he is —"

"A killer — a godless murderer —"

"But one of His people. I've heard you say that many times. All men, good or bad, are God's people and deserve —"

"I'll listen to no more of that!" York cut in, shaking his head.

He was at a loss. Back in Carlisle where he had studied for the ministry they had not prepared him for a moment such as this, when a man's own child turned from him, denying his wisdom. The essence of their training had been that given the holy inspiration and the desire, a man needed only his Bible to go forth and spread the gospel.

"And I'll not have it known that you and him —"

"Don't worry, Papa. I mean nothing to him. It's all on my side — I only wish it weren't. But if he ever asked me, I'd go with him — anywhere."

York sighed audibly. "Then I'm glad he's gone."

Sarah gave him a small smile. "He'll be back — not that it will matter for me."

"He's coming back? Where's he going if he's not leaving for good?"

"To find Yancey Lingo."

The Reverend York drew up sharply. "He knows where Yancey is?"

"I suppose so."

Ahab glanced off across the vacant stretch of land that separated the buildings of the town from the scatter of residences to the east. Rufus was probably still at home; he had seen no sign of the man on the street or in his office yet that day. He should be warned.

"Go on home, girl," he said abruptly. "I'll talk more to you later about this. I have the thought that it is time you again visited your aunt."

Sarah raised her face to him. There was a newfound independence in it now. It showed in the stubborn set of her lips, the glow in her eyes.

"I won't go —"

Harsh words sprang to York's mind but he checked them. It was not the moment to have it out, pit his parental authority against the change that had come over her and determine once and for all the winner. He must get word to Rufus Lingo.

"You will if I think it best," he said, placing his hand upon her shoulder and pushing her gently. "Now, go on home. We'll talk about it later."

Sarah moved off and Ahab York turned at once toward the house that Lingo occupied. He would relay the information Sarah had given him, tell also of seeing Starbuck load up his horse, even mention the extra coil of rope he had included; it could mean something to Rufus. He took a step, slowed, a disturbed frown on his face. What was it Sarah had said — that he was against Shawn Starbuck only because of Rufus Lingo?

Was that true? Was he, without realizing it, and for the sake of his church and congregation, turning his back upon the man? But

Starbuck was guilty of murder and Yancey was not — or at least that was the way it appeared to him, and such made a difference.

But should it? He didn't actually know Starbuck was the one who had killed Sam Culver; he was assuming it, just as was everyone, or most everyone, else in the town. York's thoughts swung to other words Sarah had flung at him — words that were his very own; *all men are God's people.* . . . Was he, in his zeal to teach the holy word, blinding himself to the truth in order to remain in the good graces of Lingo?

He was unsure. He didn't think so, but the choice was before him, one that must be made immediately; should he remain silent and thereby aid Starbuck, the one he felt was evil, or should he assist the man who had made possible the church in which he could serve his God and who continued to enrich it by his generosity?

"O Lord!" he murmured in a distracted voice as he brushed at the sweat clothing his agitated features. "Help me. If I'm doing wrong, forgive me. I want only to serve Thee!"

18

Yancey Lingo threw up his arms hurriedly, fear and surprise contorting his features. Spicer complied equally fast, but Red Davis, eyes narrowing, moved with less haste. He was the dangerous one, Shawn thought. Best to watch him closely, give him no leeway.

"On your feet — turn around!" he snapped. In the tense hush Starbuck's voice seemed to crackle. "Stand against the wall!"

The men rose, shuffled about, eyes to the back of the cabin. Shawn dropped the ropes on the table.

"What're you aiming to do?" Billy Joe asked nervously.

"Not going to kill you," Shawn replied, stepping in close, "unless you force me."

One by one he pulled their weapons from the holsters, tossed them through the doorway into the weed-littered yard. Lingo shifted anxiously.

"How'd you know where we was?"

"You left plenty of signs," Shawn answered and tapped Spicer on the shoulder. "You — step back."

Billy Joe, face chalk-white, stumbled

against a chair as he did as directed. Wheeling, he cried: "You ain't wanting me, Deputy! Was Yancey that gunned down the sheriff. Me and Red was only there. We didn't do —"

"Shut up, goddam you!" Davis snarled.

"Know all that," Starbuck said, ignoring the redhead. "Save it for now. You can tell it to the U.S. marshal when we see him." Pointing to the ropes, he added: "Want them both tied up — arms behind them. Start with Red."

Billy Joe fell to the task quickly. Finished, he looked questioningly at Shawn. Starbuck raised his free hand, shoved Davis roughly toward one of the bunks.

"Climb in. You're going to be here for a spell."

The redhead crawled awkwardly into the lower compartment of the arrangement, muttering curses, eyes glowing steadily.

"His feet," Starbuck ordered, motioning to Billy Joe. "Lash them together — tight. No tricks unless you want a grave alongside your friend Greer!"

The words served as a spur to Billy Joe. He hastily wound a length of rope around Davis's ankles, snugged it close, and completed it with a hard knot.

"Now Yancey."

Lingo lowered his arms into position. "You ain't getting away with this," he said over a shoulder. "My pa —"

"Your pa's not going to bail you out this time," Shawn cut in, waiting until Spicer had finished. "Just keep standing there — with your mouth shut."

Turning then to Spicer, he nodded. "Your turn."

Billy Joe quickly crossed his wrists behind his body. "You won't be forgetting what I told you, will you, Deputy? Was Yancey, not me or Red."

"I won't," Starbuck assured him, and holstering his pistol, bound the man's hands, and after ordering him into another of the bunks, secured his ankles.

To make doubly sure of their inability to work free, he took another length of rope, attached it to their wrists, and fastened it to the end post of the bunks.

"How long you keeping us here?" Davis asked sullenly.

"You can't let us starve!" Billy Joe added.

"Won't be for long. Might be back for you tonight, or it could be in the morning. . . . Let's go, Yancey."

"Where you taking me?" Lingo demanded, coming about.

"Jail — in Kennesaw."

Yancey's shoulders sagged with relief. A slyness came over him. "My pa'll have me out before —"

Shawn gave the man a push toward the door. "We'll see," he said and threw a final look at Davis and Billy Joe. They would be there when he returned.

Lingo, an air of confidence about him, paused as he saw his horse. "We riding double?"

"Walking until we get to the bottom of the trail. Got my sorrel picketed down there."

"Left your nag below, that it? . . . Say, how'd you get up here without us seeing or hearing you?"

"I managed," Starbuck said laconically. Jerking free the reins of Lingo's bay, and pushing Yancey on ahead, he started down the trail.

Lingo, certain in his mind of his father's power and influence, was taking the situation lightly, evidently harboring no doubt that he would be freed as soon as they reached the settlement. Such was possible, Shawn realized, unless he played it right and kept Yancey under cover until Tom Spain arrived.

He considered briefly the thought of taking Lingo to some other town — Prescott, perhaps, where there was a good jail and a lawman who was beyond Rufus Lingo's reach — but discarded it. The risk would be great, since he would be on the road for a much longer time and the possibility of encountering persons beholden to Rufus Lingo would be stronger.

Also, he was unsure of his authority. Only in Kennesaw and the county in which it lay was he a sworn deputy, and such could have a bearing, but most of all, that was where Tom Spain expected to find him.

"You're just going to a lot of trouble for nothing," Yancey said, stumbling a little over the steep grade. "Reckon you know that."

"Maybe."

"Fact is, I could fix things good for you was you to listen to some sense. You turn me loose and I'll get Pa to pay you a sort of a reward —"

Shawn laughed. "Thought you were so sure he'd get you out of this?"

"Am, but it ain't that. Just don't like you parading me into town all tied up the way I am. It'll shame me no end in front of a lot of folks I know. I got feelings."

"Didn't bother you any to kill Sam Culver."

"Was different. We was having words and he went for his gun."

162

"Not how I heard it. Happens I was standing outside the shack when you and Red and Billy Joe were talking about it."

Lingo paused, then continued on down the trail. He shrugged. "Hell, that won't mean nothing. Be your word against mine — our's — me and Pa."

"Mine and Billy Joe's and probably Red's."

"Them two? Who'll listen to them — specially Billy Joe?"

"With what I know, and it'll tie in with what he'll say, I expect a judge and a jury won't have any trouble."

"Jury! Hell, every man on one'll be a friend of Pa's. They'll do what they figure he wants them to."

"Be different in Prescott."

"What's Prescott got to do with it?"

"Expect that's where the trial will be held, since I'm turning you over to the U.S. marshal from there."

Yancey leaped into silence, the impact of Shawn's words having strong effect upon him. Near the foot of the slope, he again hesitated, half turned. The brash confidence exhibited earlier was wavering now and there was fear in his eyes.

"You sure we can't make us a deal of some kind? I'll fix you up real good — cash money and such. . . . Ain't nothing to you, anyway, far as I can see. You was no long-time friend of Sam Culver's — you scarce knew him."

"He was a man and you murdered him," Starbuck replied. "Whether he was a friend of mine or not is beside the point."

Shawn drew up abruptly. Somewhere to the east he could hear the hammer of running horses coming toward the mesa. Stepping onto a close-by rock, he threw his glance into that direction, but the rolling land with its thick stands of brush hid all from view. It could be only riders passing by — or it could be Rufus Lingo and a private posse, made aware somehow that his son's hiding place had been discovered, en route to give aid.

Stepping down, Starbuck motioned impatiently to Yancey. "Keep moving, and when you get to the bottom, cut left."

A grin split Yancey Lingo's mouth. He had heard the drum of pounding hooves, too, and reassurance had returned.

"Reckon not," he drawled, planting his feet solidly in the loose shale. "And you ain't going to be using that gun either. That'll be Pa and some of the boys coming, and if you fire a shot they'll for sure hear it."

"Probably," Starbuck said, and swung

the pistol, clublike, at Lingo's head.

It landed solidly. Yancey sagged to his knees, a look of pained surprise on his features. Holstering the weapon, Shawn leaned forward, caught the man around the waist, and threw him across a shoulder.

Moving as fast as possible, he gained the bottom of the trail, swung left, and breathing hard from the load he was carrying, hurried on. The hoofbeats were suddenly loud, and glancing toward the east, he saw Rufus Lingo and three riders break over a rise and come rushing on.

There was no time left in which to reach the sorrel, and considering the open ground that lay ahead, it would be a mistake to try anyway. At once he plunged off to the side, staggering under Yancey's weight, fairly dragging the man's bay horse behind him. Reaching a thick clump of rabbitbush, he dumped his prisoner into it, hastened to draw the bay in behind a squat cedar. Looping the leathers around a limb, he jerked off his bandana, and wheeling to the slowly arousing Lingo, fastened it tight over his mouth. Then, pistol in hand, Shawn crouched in the brush and waited for the posse to arrive.

19

There were three riders with Rufus Lingo. All were in ordinary cowhand garb, and Shawn guessed they were from his ranch. As the party drew near the foot of the trail, the land broker raised an arm, signaled a halt. There was an angry, impatient look to the man as he spoke.

"Climb off. Leave the horses here."

All dismounted. An elderly puncher with a rifle in his hand brushed at the sweat on his seamy face and stared up the slope.

"You right sure he'll be up there, Rufe?"

"Sure enough," Lingo snapped irritably. "York saw him pull out with a lot of rope hanging on his saddle. Told somebody else he was going after Yancey — and the shack's where Yancey and the other two were planning to lay out for a few days. Add it all together and what've you got?"

Shawn frowned. It was Ahab York who had tipped off Lingo, and the *somebody* mentioned was Sarah. He remembered telling her of his intentions, which were in turn passed on to her father. York had then lost no time informing Rufus Lingo. He swore softly. He should have been more careful, not given even the slightest hint of his plans to the girl, knowing that consciously or not, she would have betrayed him to her father.

But all wasn't lost. If Lingo and his men headed up the trail the chances for escaping with his prisoner and reaching Kennesaw with him were good. He could forget about Billy Joe and Red, however, insofar as being witnesses were concerned. Released, Lingo would either buy their silence or, in some way, get rid of them.

"We just going a-faunching up that trail? Sure could get a belly full of lead was he to be setting there waiting."

"He's there," Lingo said. "Figure on it. Thing to do is spread out, keep the shack covered. If you see anything move, open up."

The men all turned to him, question in their eyes. "What about Yancey — them other boys?" the older puncher asked.

"They'll have to take their chances," Lingo replied coolly.

There was a long pause. One of the other riders shrugged. "That's kind of rough on them. Why don't we wait till dark? Ain't far off."

"Be the worst thing we could do," Lingo

said, drawing his pistol. "He could hold us off easy — and he might get away."

"Get away? How?"

"Climbed up there, didn't he? Probably found a break somewhere in the cliff, made it to the top using the ropes he brought. Be just as easy to climb back down."

"Be kind of hard doing with them three on his hands."

"He'd not bother with Davis and Spicer. Probably kill them, leave them up there. It's Yancey he wants." Lingo drew back the hammer on his pistol. "Let's get started. Charlie, get over here on my left. Abe, you and Jesse string out on my right."

Shawn twisted about, hearing slight sounds of Yancey stirring. He reached out, laid a hand on the man's head, pressed him firmly back to the ground.

"Keep low," he heard Lingo warn. "And if anything up there moves, shoot."

The lives of his son and two partners meant little to the land broker, Starbuck thought as he watched the posse start up the slope. He was interested in bringing the matter of Sam Culver's murder to a close regardless of the cost. The sheriff had been right about him; he was a man with ruthless ambitions, so merciless, in fact, he was willing to sacrifice his own blood kin in order to keep the family name from being dishonored.

The party had spread into a forage line, the men spaced ten feet or so apart. Within moments, due to the steep grade, they were lost to view. Starbuck remained motionless, unwilling to move too soon for fear that he or Yancey would make a sound that would carry to Lingo and the punchers, bring them to the edge of the slope.

But he dare not tarry too long; he needed all the time possible to get his prisoner back to the settlement and hidden away. Once the posse reached the shack, found and freed Spicer and Davis, all would mount and hurry to overtake him. One thing was in his favor; as it had been pointed out, darkness was near.

He could delay no longer. Rising, Shawn caught Yancey by the arm, pulled him upright. The man was now fully conscious and close to smothering because of the tight gag covering his face. Starbuck pulled it down below his nose, refusing to remove it entirely, and heading him off along the foot of the mesa, stepped to the dense brush where the bay horse waited. Seizing the trailing reins, he led the animal into the open and fell in behind Yancey.

They reached the sorrel shortly, stopped.

Motioning Lingo to the side of his horse, Shawn took the coil of rope, as yet unused and still slung around his neck, shook out a small loop, and dropped it over his prisoner's head.

"End of this will be tied to my saddle," he said, drawing the noose fairly snug. "Just want you to know that in case you get to thinking about making a run for it. Now, mount up."

Yancey muttered something unintelligible under the gag, and with Starbuck assisting, went onto his saddle. Shawn climbed then onto his own horse, taking time to secure the end of the lariat as he had promised.

It was best they still move with care, he decided, and taking the bay's reins, he started back along the foot of the high formation. He could swing farther east but such meant breaking trail through the heat dried brush, and the resulting noise might alert Rufus Lingo and the others. It seemed wiser to stick with a beaten path.

They approached the base of the slope. Starbuck listened intently. An occasional sound was coming from somewhere near the summit — the scrape of boots, the rattle of displaced gravel. The party was almost to the shack, he guessed — which meant time was running short. He was a long way from Kennesaw.

A thought came to him. Swinging away from the trail, he pointed for the horses left behind by Lingo and the cowhands. They were bunched in a cluster of cedars, heads down, slack-hipped. He could not hope to lead all four at once, but with a little quiet persuasion, he could perhaps drift them off into the brush where they would not be so readily available.

Riding up to the animals, Shawn pulled off his hat, began to gently move them out. He was using care not to frighten them, break them into a gallop. The pound of hooves would certainly be heard up on the slope — and the one member in the party carrying a rifle just might be able to get him in his sights.

The horses responded sluggishly, stepping on their trailing reins, tossing their heads, uncertain of what it was all about. With Yancey following close behind him at the end of the rope, Starbuck kept after them until they were a good quarter mile from the mesa and then, abandoning them, doubled back to the trail. Lingo would have the horses of Spicer and Red Davis to run down the strayed mounts, of course, but it would take time, and that was what Shawn needed.

With Yancey now ahead of him, securely under control, he struck for town at a good lope. The problem that now faced him was where best to hide and wait for daylight and the arrival of Marshal Tom Spain. The jail was out of the question; it would be the first place that Rufus Lingo would look, once he and his men returned and began to search.

The hotel, the Wagonwheel Saloon, other such places where rooms were available, to each he gave full consideration and discarded all. Lingo, aided by many of the misguided townspeople, would soon ferret him out, and gunplay, something he was determined to avoid, would be inevitable.

Ahab York's church. . . .

Starbuck grinned in relief. It would be the ideal place. By the time they reached town most everyone would have retired for the night and the likelihood of someone dropping by the structure was nil. He could hold Yancey there safely until it came time to move him into a cell in the jail.

Only the saloons were lit up when they halted at the edge of town and studied the empty street. Starbuck, taking no risks, swung wide of the buildings and came in to the church from the rear. In the warm, tight hush, he drew to a stop behind the tall, narrow structure and dismounted, listening carefully for any indication that there was someone yet up and nearby.

He could hear nothing except the faint strains of piano music originating in the Wagonwheel, and stepping to Yancey's side, helped him from the saddle. Still holding to the rope that hung from the man's neck, Shawn looked about for a place to conceal the two horses. A shed at the back of a vacant house just beyond the church offered possibilities, and with Lingo in tow alongside the animals, he crossed to it.

The door was closed, and it was evident the structure had not been used in some time. Drawing back the crudely built panel, he stationed the sorrel and the bay inside. Reclosing the door, he turned and headed back for the church with the grumbling Yancey at his shoulder.

The rear entrance to the church was locked. Starbuck cursed quietly, and circled around to the front, pausing first to be certain there was no one on the street. All was clear, and crossing quickly, he tried the knob of the door. It opened, bringing a sigh of relief to Shawn. Forcing the lock would have created noise that could easily have been heard in the stillness of the night — especially by Ahab York in the parsonage only a short distance away; and the tall, gloomy minister was about the last person he wanted to encounter at that moment.

Pushing Yancey before him, he entered the church. There were windows on either side of the door, both of which would enable him to look out onto the street and observe any activity along the way. He selected the one to his left for no reason other than there were chairs handy to it.

Motioning for his prisoner to settle down in the corner, Starbuck lashed the man's ankles together, and drawing a seat close to the glass-covered opening, sank onto it. The day had been long and hard; he was both tired and hungry, but he'd have to make out for a few more hours.

20

Voices yelling in the street awoke Starbuck. He sat up with a start, glanced at his prisoner. Yancey, also awake and dimly visible in the pale light seeping through the window, lay in the corner where he had been placed. That he had tried to work himself free of the ropes that bound him was evident, but he had made no progress.

Shawn turned his attention to the street. Lingo, his search posse swelled by two, was pulling up in front of the Wagonwheel. The shouts had come from several men, probably in the act of leaving the saloon, who noted their arrival.

The church windows were closed and Starbuck could not hear what was being said, but it was a matter of small importance; he could about guess the gist of the man's words. Thoughtful, he watched the land broker lead his small army to the jail. The men spread out cautiously when they reached it, two finally making a quick dash to the door, opening it, and rushing inside. After a few moments they reappeared.

Lingo motioned toward the rear of the

building. Several of the posse, now increased in number by the men who had greeted them at the saloon, trotted around to the back, intending to have a look at the personal quarters assigned to but never occupied by him. They returned shortly, and the entire party collected in the center of the street for discussion.

More curious onlookers had come from the Wagonwheel and other saloons, some hastening to join the group, others merely standing by watching. Lingo divided his men, dispatched half to make a search along one side of the roadway, the remainder assuming responsibility for the other.

Starbuck caught occasional glimpses of them as they worked their way past the buildings, in and out of the passageways and structures that were open to them. A half hour or so later they began to reassemble, this time in the bold splash of lamplight coming from the Wagonwheel.

They had found no sign of the pair they sought, and now, stumped, were at a loss as to what next should be done. Standing in the center of the party, Rufus Lingo evidently came to the decision that Yancey and the man who held him prisoner were not in town, had instead holed up somewhere outside the limits. There was nothing to do, therefore, but wait, let Starbuck make the next move. Accordingly, everybody in the saloon for a drink on him.

The gathering broke up with a few cheers and a sudden rush for the swinging doors of the Wagonwheel. Shawn, his attention till drawn then by muffled sounds being made by Yancey, crossed to where the man lay and slipped the gag from his mouth.

"Nobody'll hear you if you yell, so don't waste your breath," he said. "All you'll get if you do is the butt of my gun again."

Yancey bobbed his head, sucked gratefully at the fresh, if trapped, warm air in the church. "Just needing to breathe," he muttered. "Was about to choke."

Starbuck returned to the window. Staying the entire night where they were would not be a good idea, he was realizing, since it would pose the problem of moving Yancey to the jail unseen that next morning. Best it be done during the night, after things quieted down. Having checked the jail once and finding it empty, Rufus Lingo was not likely to go there again.

"That was Pa and the boys, I reckon," Yancey said.

Starbuck nodded. "Had their look around and gave it up."

"Don't go betting on it. Pa won't quit till

he's found us — and when he does, why, mister, your life won't be worth a plugged copper!"

"I'll manage," Shawn said drily. "Wouldn't figure on much help from him now. He's too late."

Too late — if Tom Spain arrived in time, he amended silently. Should the federal officer fail for some reason to put in his appearance, then it would be a whole new ball of wax.

"Not for Pa. He'll fight you till you're finished. You think you can buck him here in his own town? Hell, he owns the place, and most everybody in it!"

"Maybe —"

"Ain't no maybe to it — and you sure better start listening to me or you're a dead man. I'm still willing to make you a deal. Turn me loose and I'll tell Pa to pay you a reward and let you go your way. Being dark, nobody'll ever know you been around."

"Forget it, Yancey. You murdered a man, killed him in cold blood. I aim to see you get what you deserve."

"Why? What's it to you? Like I said before, you wasn't no big friend of Sam Culver's. Me shooting him hadn't ought to bother you none. It sure ain't your business."

"Murder's everybody's business."

"Just because Culver was a damned lawman —"

"Has nothing to do with it. Point is he was a human being, and the law says no man has the right to kill another."

"You killed Harley Greer!"

"Only to stop him from gunning down Culver. . . . I'm not proud that I did it. Wouldn't have if he hadn't forced my hand."

"I don't see no difference."

"If you can't then there's no use trying to explain it to you. Truth is, men like Greer are the same as mad dogs running wild. When one stops and turns on somebody, he has to be gotten rid of."

Shawn paused. Rufus Lingo, with Davis and Billy Joe Spicer, had come out of the saloon, were walking to their horses. They mounted, swung about, and headed across the vacant lot next to the hardware store, pointing, no doubt, for the house on the east edge of town that the land broker occupied. Lingo was keeping the pair close, under his thumb. The realization drove home a second time to Shawn that the witnesses he'd hoped to use in proving Yancey's guilt had been whisked from his grasp, that it would now be a matter of convincing Tom Spain on the strength of his word and slim evidence.

Of course an attempt could be made to

force Billy Joe and the redhead to talk, but with Rufus Lingo standing back of them, willing to pay off handsomely for their silence, he could expect to gain little.

The remaining three members of the original posse pushed through the Wagonwheel's batwings and crossed to their horses. Mounting, they rode north out of town. Starbuck shifted his glance to the direction in which Lingo and Yancey's friends had disappeared. Lamplight now glowed in the windows of a house in that area.

Nodding his satisfaction, he arose, moved to the side of his prisoner. Bending over, he pulled the bandana back into place and removed the rope from the man's ankles.

"Get up — we're leaving here," he said, drawing aside.

Lingo voiced a muffled question. Shawn guessed at its meaning.

"Jail," he said.

Shepherding Yancey, Starbuck crossed to the door, opened it, and stepped out into the cool night air. Avoiding the parsonage, which lay to the left, he conducted his prisoner through the shadows to the edge of the street. Hesitating a moment to be certain no one was within visual distance, he hurriedly crossed and gained the alley behind the west row of buildings.

Moving fast but making little noise, they made their way to the jail and entered. Avoiding the lighting of any lamps, Starbuck placed his prisoner in the cell nearest to the office, removing the gag only long enough to give the man a drink before replacing it and locking the grill door.

Returning then to the front of the structure, he closed and barred the entrance to the street and settled into the chair behind the desk to wait for morning. If Marshal Tom Spain came in time all should go well; if not — Shawn tossed his hat onto the top of the desk, laid his pistol beside it — if not he'd simply have to take matters as they came.

Ahab York, slumped in the big, comfortable chair behind the pulpit that Rufus Lingo had donated for his use, sat up suddenly as voices came to him. Disturbed over the day's events, unstrung by the words Sarah had spoken, he had been unable to sleep, and rising from his bed he had pulled on his frock coat over the long nightgown he was wearing and made his way to the church.

Using the side door convenient to the parsonage, he had entered and sought out the chair. Somehow he always seemed to think better sunk deep in the worn, comfortable piece of furniture, surrounded by the peace and quiet that a man could find only inside the walls of God's house.

Now, startled, he half rose. There was somebody near the front windows. Two persons. York frowned. Drifters? Drunks? He'd had trouble before with the like, had taken to leaving the church locked up tight after the evening prayer meetings and choir practices. Lately he'd gotten out of the habit. He'd best start doing it again.

Ahab stiffened, settled back slowly into the leathery cup of the chair. The voice he'd just heard was that of that gunhand — Starbuck. . . . Something about not yelling. And then he'd heard a reply — Yancey Lingo saying it was hard to breathe.

York waited in the warm hush, not exactly certain what he should do. Simply walking down the aisle between the benches and broaching Starbuck would be foolhardy. The man wouldn't hesitate to kill him. He guessed the thing to do was remain silent, wait for an opportunity to slip back out the way he had come in and give the alarm. Such might be difficult now, however; evidently Starbuck and Yancey had been asleep when he entered. Most likely he would be heard no matter how careful he was.

"That was Pa and the boys, I reckon," he heard Yancey say.

Starbuck assured him that it was, that the search for them was being given up. York wondered how Starbuck had been able to escape Rufus and the men who had gone with him. Usually Rufus never failed in the things he undertook, but it appeared here that Starbuck had outsmarted him.

He listened to the words that were being passed between them. Yancey was trying to convince Starbuck to release him, was even offering money — a reward, he termed it. Starbuck was refusing. . . . He should try to get out, summon Rufus, Ahab thought. Perhaps if he got down on all fours, crawled . . .

"Me shooting him hadn't ought to bother you none. It sure ain't your business."

At Yancey Lingo's words Ahab York felt the blood drain from his face. Had he actually heard the boy admit to shooting Sam Culver?

"Murder's everybody's business."

Starbuck's reply burned into the Reverend York's mind in living fire. He lay back in the chair, all thoughts of escaping from the church and summoning aid leaving him. In a daze he listened to the conversation taking place in the corner of the building — Yancey protesting, threatening, begging to be freed; Starbuck firmly turning down all proposals.

Sarah had been right, he had been wrong. Starbuck had told the truth. It was Rufus who had lied — Rufus and Yancey, and blindly, he had fallen in with the lie and given his support to them.

Maybe what Sarah had said about his feelings toward Rufus Lingo was true. He hadn't looked at it that way, though. He'd simply believed in the man and was grateful for all the help that had been forthcoming to the church. And there was to be more; the new organ to replace the old piano that was worn out when it was given to them, the fine gumwood pews that Rufus had mentioned, the supply of extra hymn books that would enable every member of the congregation to have one for his own use instead of three or four of them crowding about to sing from one.

But he could forget all that if he made known what he had heard Yancey admit. It would be the end of the flow of gifts from Rufus Lingo, the precious, much-needed items that his people so wanted and that were responsible to a great extent for the steady increase in the church's membership.

Again he was faced with choice. He saw

that clearly. He could remain silent, never speak of the words he had overheard, and the horn of plenty would continue to provide, the church flourish. He could tell of what Yancey had said, verify all that Starbuck had maintained, and the son of Rufus Lingo would then be convicted of murder. Thus justice would be served — but at the expense of God's house and His people.

Which? Should he think first of the law or of God's work? Which was the more important? Should he serve God and His people or the forces of law and order? Should he deny himself, all that he believed in, all the words he had uttered affirming truth and honesty and the adherence to God's commandments, for the sake of his church?

"Get up — we're leaving here. . . . Jail."

It was Starbuck. York leaned forward. In the half-dark he could see the silhouettes of the two men crossing to the door, the brief spurt of light as it was opened and quickly closed.

They were gone. Torn, troubled, Ahab York slid forward in his chair and sank to his knees. Clasping his big hands, he lowered his head and again beseeched his Maker for guidance.

21

Starbuck awoke by sunrise. Stiff, sore from a night in the slatted chair, he got to his feet, moved about in the confines of the small office to loosen his muscles. Then, after dousing his face and head from water in the bucket, he turned to the inner door for a look at his prisoner. Yancey Lingo was sprawled on the cot in his cell, still asleep.

Closing the heavy panel, Shawn crossed to the window, drew the shade aside, and glanced into the street. A few persons were up and abroad, most of them merchants preparing their stores for the day's business. He could see no one in Rufus Lingo's office, guessed the land broker had not yet come from his home. When he did Spicer and Davis would be with him; he would want them around close by.

Pulling back, Starbuck paused. It was already hot, and the room, shut up tight, had a stale, musty odor. He'd like to open the door, or at least one of the windows, and let it air out, but he'd best forget it. The people of Kennesaw, and Rufus Lingo, thought the jail unoccupied; it was best to let them keep

186

on thinking that as long as possible. Once U.S. Marshal Spain was on hand it would be a different matter, but until then he would have to lie low with his prisoner.

He should arrange it so he could watch the street unnoticed, however. He gave that a few moments' consideration, and then drawing his knife, stepped back to the roller shade pulled over the window. Leaving it as it was, he slit a six-inch gash in the thick oil-cloth fabric, near its top, thus providing himself with a port through which he could look out upon the town and yet be unseen.

Testing the arrangement, he again surveyed the street. Three riders were approaching town, coming across the flat to the east. It was Lingo and Yancey's two friends. They were heading, no doubt, for the land broker's office. Back up the way Doc Grey had halted to speak with a woman carrying a market basket, and on beyond them Shawn could see the Reverend York moving about in front of the church.

That drew a frown to his face. If the minister should happen to get near the shed of the vacant house nearby he would likely discover the horses inside it. Identifying them, especially Yancey's bay, would result quickly, and the word would be out that he and Lingo's son were somewhere in town.

After a moment Starbuck shrugged. There was nothing he could do about it — and the fact would become known eventually anyway. He was only hopeful of delaying that moment until the federal peace officer arrived.

He was depending heavily upon Tom Spain, Shawn realized. Perhaps too heavily. There was the chance that his letter had gone undelivered, that the lawman was out of town when the stagecoach driver reached Prescott; or it could be that he was involved in other important matters from which it was impossible to take leave.

If such proved to be the fact, then what? He just couldn't continue to stay holed up in the jail with Yancey, without food and water, waiting for the lawman to come. It would never go that far, he realized in the next instant. Their presence in the jail would be discovered, and Rufus Lingo, with the help of the townspeople, would storm the place to recover his son, and before he would engage in any gunplay with them, Shawn knew he would surrender his prisoner.

Were Yancey convicted, awaiting execution, it would be a different situation; he would be obligated to hold the man at all costs. But since he was only suspect in the eyes of the law, and the proof of guilt was the word of a man no longer a deputy insofar as the town was concerned, he had little grounds to go to extremes. He was on thin ice, and if a crack appeared ahead, he could do nothing but back off.

Wheeling, Starbuck returned to the adjoining room, in which the cells stood. Yancey was unusually quiet, and that stirred suspicion within him; before that moment he would have expected the man to be raising a clamor of sorts for food and water.

Crossing to the grill of bars, he looked into it. Lingo still slept. He had rolled over, now lay face down. His hands were still securely bound, and the gag across his mouth appeared to be in place. Satisfied, Shawn retreated into the office and to his lookout post at the window.

The hard pound of running horses greeted him. He swung his attention to the lower end of the street. It was the eastbound stage. He drew up with interest, watched the careening vehicle sweep by, slide to a halt in a cloud of swirling dust in front of the hotel. If Tom Spain was coming by coach, he would be on this one.

The curved door swung open. A man stepped forward from the group of bystanders on the porch of the hostelry, extended his arms, and assisted a woman to alight. . . . His wife or a visiting relative, Shawn supposed. No one else descended, and the driver, luggage of the departing passenger dragged from the boot and deposited on the board sidewalk, was climbing back to his perch. The lawman had not been aboard.

Disappointed, Starbuck started to turn away, hesitated. Crossing the street was Sarah York. Behind her, carrying a small bag, was Ahab. Wondering, Shawn watched the tall minister hand the girl up into the coach, pass the bag to her, and step back. Sarah was leaving. She had made no mention of such to him that day before when they talked. It had been a brief conversation, to be sure, but if she had known then that she was going away, he was certain she would have told him.

The stage lurched forward, dust streamers spilling from its iron-tired wheels as it picked up speed. Shawn followed it with his gaze until it had rounded the corner and was lost to view, and then drew back, a dull feeling of loss stirring through him. Sarah had awakened something within him, a different interest, a feeling he had never before experienced. It was odd that in this one solitary incident he had been unable to do anything about it.

Shrugging, accepting it as something beyond his control, he shifted his thoughts to Tom Spain. The fact that the lawman was not on the coach did not necessarily mean he was not coming; he could be riding in on horseback, or, for that matter, he could have already arrived, since sufficient time had elapsed for him to make the trip. But a growing doubt was now filling Starbuck, and with each passing minute the belief that he would be compelled to face the final confrontation alone became stronger. He shook his head; best he assume that to be the case and make whatever preparations he could — or should.

Recrossing the office to the cellblock, he looked in again on Yancey Lingo. The man yet lay on the cot, face now turned to the wall. He was snoring gently, seemingly having no worries about the future, certain in mind that his parent would eventually extricate him from his predicament. He might not be resting so confidently had he been conscious at the time and overheard the orders his father had given to the rescue posse at the mesa, Shawn thought wryly.

Once again in the office, Starbuck considered the rack of shotguns and rifles affixed to the wall behind the desk. The key to the lock and chain securing them was on the ring lying before him but he made no move to use it, still determined to employ only reason and not resort to gunfire.

He had but one course he could follow — wait until it was obvious that Tom Spain was not coming, noon perhaps, and then simply open the door to the jail. Such would be a signal to all, especially Rufus Lingo, whose business quarters were almost opposite, that he was there, and logically, Yancey as well.

He could expect the townspeople, headed by the elder Lingo, the councilmen, and Reverend York, to bear down upon him quickly, demand the release of his prisoner. He would make a final attempt to convince them that they would be freeing a killer, and when that failed, he'd have no option other than to accede to their ultimatum. In so doing he would have failed the law insofar as —

A sudden yell coming from the adjoining cellroom brought Starbuck around sharply. It was Yancey's voice, loud and shrill as it broke the morning hush.

"Help! It's Yancey — the deputy's got me locked up in here! Somebody get my pa!"

Shawn wheeled, taut with anger, halted. Lingo had managed somehow to slip his gag, and by standing on the end of the cot, had shouted his message through the small barred window high in the wall. His voice would have carried to everyone along the street — and it was too late now to do anything about it.

Grim, Starbuck came about, stepped up to the door, and removing the bar, drew it open. . . . As well be now as noon.

22

Starbuck framed himself in the opening. Several men were moving toward the jail, among them Dolan, the Reverend York, and Pete Whitcomb of the Wagonwheel. As they drew abreast the hotel they were joined by others who were standing on the porch.

Two members of the impromptu delegation broke clear and were hurrying toward Rufus Lingo's office, anxious no doubt to be the first bringing news to him of his son's whereabouts. Glancing to the broker's quarters, Shawn could see him, flanked by Red Davis and Billy Joe Spicer, behind the window, looking out. As the couriers trotted up, Lingo jerked open the door. There was a moment's hasty discourse, after which all of the men came streaming across the street to the jail.

"I want Yancey —"

Rufus Lingo voiced his peremptory demand almost before he had halted. The others closed in around him, Davis and Billy Joe at either elbow, the townspeople and curious bystanders to the sides.

"Not till I've had my say," Starbuck replied coolly, conscious of the building tension.

"That's something you ain't got around here no more," Dolan stated, pushing forward a step. "Council took that away from you."

"Could be," Shawn countered, "but that won't change the fact that the man I've got locked up inside is guilty of murder."

"You can't prove it," the merchant said.

"Heard him admit it, and Spicer there was ready to talk about it. Had him and Davis trussed up for witnesses, but Lingo and his men turned them loose. Yancey was hiding up in a shack on a mesa. They were with him."

"Weren't hiding," Rufus Lingo declared. "They went up there to do a little drinking — you know why. Man you killed was their friend."

"Expect you sent them there — same as I figure you know he shot down Sam Culver. You lied about the time that Yancey and the others left town. You had a reason for that."

The crowd in the street had grown larger. Starbuck let his glance run over it, touch the face of each person present. Except for Nella, standing a bit apart from the rest, he read nothing but hostility and threat.

"I know Yancey murdered the sheriff. Admitted it to me. So did Spicer. All I'm asking is that you let things stand until the U.S. marshal gets here from Prescott. I'll leave it up to him — if he thinks there's proof enough to hold Yancey for trial, well and good. If not, I'll step aside and he can go free."

"Supposing we don't want to wait?" a voice, belligerent and pressing, asked from the front of the group.

"Now, no need to talk about force," Rufus Lingo said, raising his hands to still the sudden hubbub. "I can clear this up right now." Turning to Spicer, he said, "Billy Joe, did you tell the deputy that Yancey shot the sheriff?"

"No, sir, I purely didn't."

"You ever hear Yancey admit it to him?"

"Sure didn't, Mr. Lingo. The deputy's lying."

The land broker faced Davis. "How about you?"

The redhead shrugged. "I didn't hear nothing."

Lingo made a gesture of conclusion. "There, I expect that will lay to rest any doubt some of you might have. These boys and Yancey had nothing to do with the murder. I imagine it's just the way we figured at first; Starbuck is simply trying to cover his own tracks. . . . To my way of thinking, if you want Sam Culver's killer, you ought to be locking him up."

There was a sudden shifting in the crowd, a quick mutter of voices. From the fringe a tall, sparsely built man in a trim business suit moved into the clear. Sharp-faced, with dark, close-set eyes, clipped mustache, and pointed goatee, he walked with the short, mincing steps of a man more accustomed to the saddle than the sidewalk.

Reaching the front of the jail, he paused on the stoop, turned to the gathering. "The name's Spain," he said, drawing back the front of his coat to reveal the badge pinned to his shirt pocket. "I'm the U.S. marshal."

A fresh wave of murmurs rolled through the group. Shawn stared at the man. "How long've you been here?" he asked in a low voice.

"Last night — late."

Anger flooded Starbuck. "Would've appreciated knowing that," he said stiffly. "We could have talked this over a bit."

"Two pretty good reasons why we didn't," Spain replied quietly. "Didn't know where you were. Jail was empty when I got here — and I wanted to hear the other side of the story. You got anything to add to what you put in your letter — proof of some kind?"

"Only what you heard me say about Spicer and Davis."

The lawman shook his head. "Won't help. . . . Far as I'm concerned you're telling the truth about it. Can expect them to lie."

The people in the street were silent as they looked on, undoubtedly wondering at the low conversation that was taking place between the two men. Rufus Lingo's patience finally came to an end.

"I'm the boy's father," he said, making it sound almost as if Yancey was a youngster caught in a crime no greater than stealing apples. "Since you are in authority here now, I insist you turn him loose at once."

Tom Spain's dark eyes flickered. "Insist is a strong word, mister — and I'm not in charge unless I decide to take over. Starbuck is the law here."

"We fired him!" Dolan shouted angrily.

"You can't," the marshal answered in his quiet, unperturbed way. "Before riding over I talked about this with the officials in Prescott, showed them the letter I'd received from him —"

"You got a letter from him — from Starbuck?" Lingo said in a surprised tone.

Spain nodded. "A full report on Sam Culver's murder along with the details of your taking away his commission. Happens you didn't have the authority. Culver was an elected official, paid by all of the people in this county, not just by you. He appointed Starbuck and that puts him in the same position. Was told the only man able to revoke his appointment under the circumstances is the governor."

Dolan retreated into the crowd. Lingo, however, his habitual façade of genteelness cracking visibly, shook his head, swore.

"All right, so he's still the deputy. Doesn't change the fact that he's got my son locked up in there for something you can't prove he did!"

The lawman's shoulders stirred faintly. "Have to admit you're right, although, for my money, he probably is guilty but we can't prove it. I've had word before, from Culver, about this son of yours, and in my opinion he should have been behind bars a long time ago. But the way the law works, it protects somebody like him while not meaning to."

Lingo's face was expressionless. "That mean you're turning him loose?"

"No choice," Spain said wearily, shaking his head at Shawn. "We know plenty — can't prove anything —"

"I can give you the proof, Marshal —"

At the words, everyone wheeled to Ahab

York. Tom Spain brushed his wide-brimmed hat to the back of his head, frowned. Starbuck came forward a step. Rufus Lingo, features dark and furious, only stared.

"Who're you, mister?"

"Name's York. I'm the minister of the Holy Writ Church."

The federal lawman folded his arms across his chest. "You know something about this matter?"

York flung a despairing look at the land broker, brought his eyes back to Spain. "I know Yancey Lingo's guilty. Heard him admit it last night."

"Heard him — where?"

"In my church. The deputy brought him there to hide, then moved him here to the jail after everybody had quit searching for them. They were talking — didn't know I was around."

"You expect anybody to believe that?" Lingo shouted.

"I don't lie, not about anything," York said, his usually booming voice low and restrained. "Perhaps I've been a bit blind for what I thought was good reason, and I no doubt have other shortcomings, but I don't lie."

Rufus Lingo was suddenly trembling with

anger. He whirled on the minister. "You — you'd do this to me after all I've done for your damned church!"

"A man has to stand up for right, no matter what it costs him — or his people," York said, looking away. "I'm grateful for your favors, but God will not permit me to lie for the sake of them."

The crowd was in shocked silence. From somewhere in its depths a man said: "Well, reckon that tears it."

Tom Spain turned to Starbuck, smiled. "Seems we've got our proof — and a witness."

Shawn nodded. "Glad it worked out. Don't like to think of a murderer being turned loose. Like as not you won't have any trouble now getting Spicer and Red Davis to talk."

"Probably won't, unless the lawyer the boy's pa is sure to hire manages to get them out of the country. Won't make too much difference. That preacher — he's all we'll need." The lawman paused, extended his hand. "Owe you some thanks for what you did."

Shawn glanced out over the sullen, withdrawn crowd. It was beginning to break up and drift off. Only Nella had not stirred and showed a proud, congratulatory smile to him.

"Was my job," he said. "Far as I was concerned I was still Sam Culver's deputy."

Riding slowly toward the parsonage that next morning, gear strapped to the sorrel and ready for the trail, Starbuck gave Kennesaw a thoughtful survey. The hostility toward him had not lessened, and he'd be glad to leave the place behind. The majority of the townspeople, as children deprived of something unwholesome and blaming the benefactor for its loss, resented him.

He viewed the paradox with resignation. He had simply done what he believed was necessary, and the law had been served. Yancey was already on the way to Prescott with Tom Spain, where he would stand trial. Rufus Lingo, finally admitting to the facts, was making a show of recovering his status by declaring that if his son were indeed guilty, he should be punished.

He came abreast the church, swung into the yard. Ahab York, apparently at the window of the small bungalow that served as home, came out at once, his elongated face solemn as he watched Shawn pull to a stop.

"Never got a chance to thank you for speaking up yesterday," Starbuck said, resting an elbow on the saddlehorn. "I know how much that cost you."

York's wide shoulders twitched. "To have not would have been as great a sin as to falsely accuse. As for the cost, God will provide."

"Expect so. Anyway, I'm obliged. Would've hated to see a murderer go free." Shawn hesitated, then, "I saw Sarah leave. When she returns give her my regards and say I'll see her again someday."

Ahab York drew himself up stiffly. "I sent her away to keep her from you," he said coldly. "She's not your kind, Starbuck — you've got to understand that. She has been raised in the ways of the Lord. You are a man from a different world, a man who has killed, justly perhaps, but killed nevertheless, and thus there is blood on your hands. . . . Sarah is not for you."

Shawn studied the tall man quietly for a moment, the faintest trace of a smile on his lips. "I suppose not," he murmured, and wheeled the sorrel about.

Reaching the gate, he cut back into the street, looked again at the rows of weathered buildings, their dusty windows mirroring and flattening the sunlight. It was the past now; Sarah, the Lingos, Nella, Sam Culver, Ahab York — all were slowly becoming shadows and taking their places with others already in the background of memory. . . . Only finding Ben remained distinct and important.

We hope you have enjoyed this Large Print book. Other Thorndike Press or Chivers Press Large Print books are available at your library or directly from the publishers.

For more information about current and upcoming titles, please call or write, without obligation, to:

Thorndike Press
P.O. Box 159
Thorndike, Maine 04986 USA
Tel. (800) 223-1244 or (800) 223-6121

OR

Chivers Press Limited
Windsor Bridge Road
Bath BA2 3AX
England
Tel. (0225) 335336

All our Large Print titles are designed for easy reading, and all our books are made to last.